If It Don't Kill You...

Tanika M. Fears

ISBN:978-1-7356743-2-2

Cover Designed byKozakura
Manuscript Edited by Tara Parrish
Library of Congress Control: 2020923261

DEDICATION

This book is dedicated to my mother Rosemary Fears. She is my inspiration; I don't think she knew that she was my hero. Her strength, courage and resilience taught me that nothing is impossible. She was the first author I knew she would read me poems and short stories that she had written, but never published, this book is for her dreams thar went unfilled and all the untold stories she was unable to publish.

CONTENTS

ACKNOWLEDGMENTS

I would like to thank my children; their support has been my motivation to write and publish my book. To my dear friends who have been there from the first word written, thank you for your prayers and support

1 CHAPTER

I sat at my desk staring at the calendar as if the date was somehow wrong; unfortunately, it wasn't. This very day one year ago, June 1, 2015, my whole life as I knew it was changed forever. That day would have started like any other day, but my husband Jason didn't come home the night before. I woke the twins up trying not to worry or get upset. The only other time Jason had stayed out all night was when he cheated on me, but that was five years ago. There were a few other reasons why he may not have come home, and those were the reasons I really didn't want to think about. Just as I was about to make breakfast, the phone rang. My heart was beating fast as I reached for the phone. I was relieved when I heard Tee's voice—she was Jason's best friend and partner in crime.

All I could get out was a hello and she started talking, "Why is your husband dodging me? I've been calling his cell since last night!"

Now I was really beginning to worry. I was calling him all night as well, I told her, and he didn't come home last night. She quickly started reassuring me that everything was OK, that maybe he was at his mother's house. Tee was there through the whole cheating ordeal, so she was trying to do damage control, but I wasn't thinking about him cheating. Before I told her what I was thinking, I looked up the stairs to make sure the twins weren't coming down. As the words came out, I felt this sick feeling in the pit of my stomach. I said it quickly, "Tee, could Jason be in jail?" but she quickly said, "No."

Before Tee could say another word, my other line clicked; I clicked over hoping it was Jason. It wasn't Jason, it was Chase. Jason and I grew up with Chase, but I hadn't spoken to him in years. Last I heard, he was a detective for the Saint Paul Police Department. He asked if it would be OK if he stopped by; he wanted talk to me about something. I was starting to feel dizzy—I can't explain it, but I felt sick like I was coming down with the flu. I told Chase that would be fine, and I clicked back over in a daze.

I told Tee that Chase was coming over and said he had something he needed to talk to me about. She didn't say anything thing at first, so I said it louder, "Did you hear me? Chase is on his way!" With her voice cracking, she said, "Shit, Leia, you might be right. Jason could've gotten picked up. Chase always looks out for us; he tells us when shit was hot on

2

the streets. So, if there's any problem, he's got Jason's back. Call me as soon as he leaves."

I hung up with her and called my Nana. I asked her could she take the kids to day camp if Jason was in jail. I didn't want them finding out right now. They had no idea what their father did for a living, and I wanted it to stay that way for now. Jada came down first and I hoped she didn't ask where her dad was. She walked up to me and put her hand on my shoulder and said, "Mom, is everything OK? You look upset?" I looked at her and all I could do was lie. "I am fine, Sweetheart, just a little tired." She sat at the table and asked, "Is Dad picking us up after camp?" I was thinking if Jason was in jail, the kids should stay the night at Nana's. If he didn't come home again, they would have too many questions.

I sat next to Jada and replied, "You know I was thinking you and your brother should stay the night at Nana's. I have a lot to do, and I need some peace and quiet." Her smile quickly turned into a frown, and she started talking with her pouty voice, "Mom, you know Nana has no cable except church channels, she doesn't like us to use the phone and on top of that no sweets and we have to go to bed at 8:30 p.m."

I put my arm around her shoulder and told her "Jada I know, but I really need this time to myself." She stood up and headed upstairs. She stormed up a few steps and turned and yelled "Yeah right, you and daddy are probably planning one of your date nights!"

I wish that were the case: at that point I was just saying silent prayers that everything would be all right. Lil' Jay came down and Jada must have broken the news to him about their sleepover and he wasn't very happy, either. He came and stood in front of me with the same frown and pouty voice as Jada. "Mom, where's Dad? He said after camp he would take me to get some shoes."

I couldn't believe Jason told Lil' Jay that he was getting a new pair of shoes; he just bought him a pair last week. I was trying to hide the fact that I was upset, so I smiled and said, "First of all, you don't need a new pair of shoes. You already have way too many shoes!" Lil' Jay was in full brat mode at this point. "Dad has twice the amount that I have, and Jada has more than me!" This boy doesn't really think I'm going to cave with that line, but I had too much on my mind to go back and forth with him right now. I gave him a ray of hope, "Fine, Jay, we'll see. I need to talk to your dad, and I'll call you at Nana's."

Before Jay could say another word, the bell rang I was glad because I was starting to lose my mind. I wanted to know what happened and what it would take to fix it.

I was so glad to see Nana; she always makes me feel better. I gave her a big hug, "Good morning, Nana." She had a worried look on her face she pulled me to the side. I know she knew something was wrong—she knew what Jason did for a living and she didn't like it, but she never treated Jason badly because of it. Nana is saved, but she would always say that "only God can judge him." She whispered, "Is everything OK, Leia?"

I sighed and whispered back, "I'm not sure. Chase called this morning and said he wanted to stop by to talk about something… I think Jason might have gotten into trouble last night." She squeezed my arm and said, "Don't think of this as a bad thing, Leia, this might be a blessing. Jason has never had to take responsibility for what he's doing, so if he did get caught, maybe that will bring an end to this hustling stuff!" I wasn't thinking about it like that; maybe she was right. If Jason did get caught—and God forbid he had to go to jail—maybe that would make him see that it wasn't worth it.

I gave Nana another hug and whispered, "Maybe you're right, Nana. This just might be the end of his street life. Thank you." I told her that the kids would be staying overnight, and unlike the twins, she was very happy. She enjoyed having them around.

After they left, I started cleaning the kitchen, and as soon as I was about to change the doorbell rang. Shit, I didn't want Chase to see me looking crazy! I tried to fix myself up as best I could on my way to the door. When I opened the door, Chase was standing there looking very solemn. He reached out his hand and said, "How are you?"

I was confused because we hadn't seen each other in years, but we weren't on a formal level. I took his hand and greeted him, "I'm fine, thank you." Chase came in and followed me into the living room and I offered him some orange juice because I knew he hated coffee. I went and got his glass of orange juice, and when I came back in the living room his demeanor went from solemn to somber.

I handed Chase the glass and sat down across from him. Chase took an unusually long drink and then sat for a minute looking down at the cup in his hand. I can't explain it, but at that moment I knew Jason was coming home. Chase looked at me and now he had tears in his eyes. He got up and came and sat next to me on the loveseat, took my hands and then took a deep breath. My heart began beating so hard I thought it was going to break out of my chest. He looked at me and said, "Leia, this is very hard for me to have to tell you, "He stopped to clear his throat. Tears started rolling down his face. I didn't need him to finish, because my heart knew what he was trying to say. This was the worst-case scenario that I had played out in my head a million times. Chase squeezed my hands hard and looked up and said, "Leia, Jason is gone"

I sat there for a moment and for some reason what he said wouldn't register. It was like my heart knew but my mind wouldn't accept it. I snatched my hand back and stood up and snapped at him, "What do you mean, Chase? What are you saying?" He stood up and took my hands again and repeated, "Leia, Jason is gone. I am so sorry!"

I fell in his arms screaming and wailing, "Oh my God, this isn't happening! No, not Jason! I cried while Chase asked if I wanted him to call Jason's mother, but I knew I had to be the one to tell her myself. I told him no and wiped my tears. As hard as it was to hear, I knew it was going to be harder to say. But I knew that I had to be the one to tell Sandra. I called her and asked her to come over right away. She wanted to know what was going on, but I wouldn't tell her; I didn't want to tell her over the phone. I wanted to be there for her, and I needed her to be there for me.

Chase waited with me as I called Nana next. By the time I dialed the number, I was crying so hard I didn't even hear her answer the phone. All I could hear was Nana yelling, "Leia, baby, calm down! What's wrong?" The words came out in between the tears, "Nana he's gone; Jason is gone!" That was all I could get out before the tears started again.

I could hear the sorrow in Nana's voice, "Oh my Lord, Leia! I know that there isn't anything I can say to make this easier for you but in

Matthew 5:4 it says, 'Blessed are those who mourn, for they will be comforted.' When you feel at your weakest, find comfort in the Lord."

I thanked her and I made sure to tell her not to let the kids watch the news. A black man found dead would surely make the 10 o'clock news, and I didn't want them to find out that way. I called Tee next. I wanted to call her before Sandra got here to tell her that Jason wasn't in jail, but instead it was the worst thing that we could have imagined. Tee has been Jason's best friend since they were 15 years old Jason's mother Sandra and his Uncle James didn't like her because she's gay, and most older people couldn't grasp that.

As the phone rang, I tried to pull it together, but I couldn't. She answered and I just said it, "Tee, Jason's not in jail. They found his body this morning. He's gone, Tee!" All I could hear was my crying.

Then I heard her weeping for just a second, then she said she was on her way. I sat there not saying anything to Chase. I was in a daze; yesterday was perfect. Jason had taken me and the kids to dinner to celebrate my last class, which meant that I was finally getting my master's degree. After dinner, he dropped us off at home, and said he was only going to be gone an hour or so. I wish I would have made Jason stay home.

Sandra came in the house looking worried and sat down between Chase and me. She could tell something was wrong. My eyes felt big and swollen and I could feel myself trembling. I took her hands and when I looked at her, I could see fear in her eyes. That broke my heart even more. Jason was the love of my life, my best friend and my husband, but he was Sandra's child. I spoke quietly as if that would soften the blow. "Sandra, I'm so sorry Jason's gone." The impact of the words hit her like a brick.

She fell over and was screaming, "Oh Lord, not my baby! Why my son?" I sat her up and held her and we both cried; it felt like someone was pulling my heart out. I kept trying to stop, but I couldn't. The pain was so familiar—it was the same pain I felt when I lost my father. After a while we both calmed ourselves so that we could try to make sense of it all and just then Tee came. I've never seen Tee cry and I could tell she had been crying. She stood in the doorway looking sad, but not saying a word.

"Chase, what happened to my son?" Sandra said in a whisper. Chase looked over at Sandra and said, "He was shot, Mrs. Robertson." Sandra gasped and started crying again. I just sat there thinking that this must be a nightmare. Jason didn't have any enemies—at least none that I knew of. Chase interrupted my thoughts, "I know that this is still a shock, but I need one of you to come to Holy Angels Hospital to identify the body." Sandra answered him before I could say a word "We'll all go. Please just give me a second; I need to call my husband."

Sandra went in the other room to call Albert, and I was still sitting there, now mad at myself for not doing enough to make Jason stop selling drugs. I would bring it up from time to time, but he would always say the timing wasn't right. To be honest, I guess I never pushed because I was scared if I made him choose, he'd choose the street life. It was like he was addicted to it. Now here I was, a widow at 28 and no clear understanding as to why. Out of nowhere Tee started talking and Chase and I both looked up, even though it felt like she was just talking aloud.

"Jay was the only real friend I had; the only person that didn't judge me. He accepted me for who I was, and now someone has taken that friend away." Then she looked at me and said with this tone that stuck with me, "Leia, do you still believe in God?" I knew Tee didn't believe in God. I used to always tell her that you can't blame God for all that's wrong in the world, but she wasn't hearing that. I also knew she was afraid of God because she thought God hated her for being gay. I wasn't about to have this conversation now, so I ignored her question.

Just then Sandra came back in the living room, and we all got ready to go to the hospital. Chase suggested we ride with him. On the way, there I just kept saying to myself maybe this is all a mistake. Once we got there it wouldn't be Jason, and all could go back to normal.

We pulled up to the hospital and I felt a knot in my stomach. I took a deep breath and then we got out. Once we were inside, my heart was beating so fast I felt like I was going to pass out. Just as I was about to lose it, Sandra took my hand and we walked into the morgue together.

Chase stopped and turned to us, and it was at that moment that I realized I couldn't do this. I wasn't strong enough for this. I backed away from Sandra and Chase, held my hands up, and shook my head saying out loud what I was thinking in my head. "I am sorry, but I can't do this. I need to go outside I feel like I can't breathe."

Sandra came and took my hands and gently said, "Leia, you can do this and you're not alone. I am here and we'll get through this together."

I looked in Sandra's eyes, took a deep breath and we followed Chase into the room. It was cold and dark-feeling, and I got the chills as soon as we walked in. There is no other way to explain it, but it smelled like death in that room. Then we went through another door and in the middle of the room there was a sliver table with a body on it covered with a white sheet. I stopped because this feeling came over me that I can't explain. I felt Jason. Not like he was dead, but how I would know when he entered the room without looking up. The tears started rolling down my face.

When the coroner asked if we were ready, we both looked at each other and shook our heads yes. He pulled the sheet down and there he was, laying there with the saddest look on his face. Seeing him like that broke my

heart. Jason was always smiling, even when he was mad. He told me once

that he practiced that so even when he was pissed off, no one would know.

He said it was a defense mechanism he needed for the streets so that when

he had drama the other person wouldn't be able to read him or tell when he

was going to make his move.

Sandra was holding his hand crying and praying all at the same

time. I just stood there looking at him and the tears started falling on his

beautiful face. I softly rubbed them away. I laid my head on his chest like I

always did and started talking to him. "Baby, I need you. Why is this

happening? Why do you have to leave me now? How I am I supposed to

live in a world that doesn't include you?" Then I fell to my knees to plead

with God. "Please God, let this be a mistake! I know you have the power to

raise the dead. Please bring him back! Please, God!"

Sandra kneeled beside me and said, "Leia, honey, please get up. I

think we should go; you need to lay down." I stood up and laid my head

back on his chest and wrapped my arms around him. I heard Sandra telling

me we had to go, but I couldn't leave him like this. I turned and looked at

Sandra and wiped my tears a told her, "No, Sandra I have to stay with him.

Who's going to be here with him? I won't leave him here alone!"

Sandra looked at me then put her arm around my shoulder and whispered, "I know this is hard for you because it's tearing me up inside, but I know he's with God, so he'll be all right. "I looked at her and at that moment I was angry with her. How in the world could she say he's all right? He's lying on this table, dead!

I just held on to him, sobbing…I couldn't let go. I heard and felt Sandra and Chase trying to get me to leave, but I just couldn't. I remember closing my eyes, opening them again, and the room started spinning. The next thing I remembered was waking up in my bed.

I looked up and Nana was sitting in the chair next to my bed, reading her Bible. She looked over at me and I shook my head and said, "I was hoping I would wake up and it all would have been a nightmare!" Nana got up and sat next to me and said, "No baby, it was real. I know sometimes life can feel like a nightmare."

I sat up and looked at the clock and it was 9:30 p.m. I asked Nana, "Where are the twins? They don't know, do they?" Nana took my hand and replied, "Don't worry they're fine, and no they don't know. I dropped them off with your mother." That totally threw me off and I asked "What? They're at Mother's?" Nana looked at me and smiled and said "Yes, I thought it was about time she helped out. She is their grandmother."

I dropped my body back on the bed and said, "Nana, I don't think I can handle this. When I lost daddy, I thought I wouldn't ever feel secure again. When I met Jason, he made me feel safe and secure. Now I just feel empty."

Nana rubbed her hand across my head and kissed my forehead and said, "You're in mourning and it takes you through so many different emotions that you think you going to lose your mind. So long as you don't shut down and shut people out, you'll make it through this, I promise."

Then she held me while I wept. When I woke up again, it was morning I got up and looked out my window that overlooked my garden. Every morning, I'd stand in the window and Jason would get up and wrap his arms around me. That would never happen again. All the love and support that he gave me was gone, and I was alone to raise our children. How can this be happening? I've loved this man since I was thirteen how do I let go how do I get over this?

My graduation ceremony is in a few weeks. How could I go without Jason? He was the one who supported me through my B.A. and then my master's. I had planned on surprising him and giving him the rest of the trust fund that daddy had set up for me. It was my way to say thank you for supporting my dreams, and now let me support yours. I wanted him to stop making excuses and stop hustling. The money would have been enough for him to go to business school and start his construction company.

I stood there going over all the mistakes I made and being mad at myself for not doing everything I could to ensure that Jason would always be here with us. I went in and got in the shower. I knew the whole family would be here, plus Chase wanted to talk to Sandra and I. Nana thought it was too soon, but I wanted to get it over with. I also wanted to know what happened.

As soon as I got dressed, Sandra was knocking on the door. "Honey, everyone is here!" I took a deep breath and followed her downstairs. Everyone was in the living room waiting for me: Jason's Uncle James who is also my best friend's dad, his half-brothers Jordan and Jacob, his cousin Oliver, his stepfather and two of his cousins. Then there were my cousins Nate, Robert, Chris and Anna. my half-brother Lance, and my mother. They were all hugging me and asking me was I OK, and if I needed something, to let them know. I know they meant well, but I just wanted to meet with Chase and go back upstairs.

My mother said she would pick up the twins from Nana and keep them another night so that I could rest. That was surprising—they're 13, and last night was the first time she's ever kept them or spent any real time with them. I walked over and gave my mother a hug and told her, "Thank you for the offer, but they need to know." She quickly responded, "Leia, you need time to yourself. They'll be fine."

It was just like her to try to control the situation. I wanted them to know; it's already been two days. Jason and I were always open and honest with the twins about everything, except for Jason's line of work. I was 15 when I got pregnant with the twins and when my mother found out, she gave me two options: get an abortion or leave her house. I moved in with Nana until Jason could buy us a house.

My mother didn't even so much as look at me when I was in church. She would sit in the back or when I would see her in the neighborhood, she would act as if she didn't see me. It wasn't until I was giving birth to the twins that Nana had to call her. I was having some complications and there were some forms my mother had to fill out. She showed up taking control, insisting that she be in the room even though I said I didn't want her to be. I thought she was coming around, but she wasn't.

After that, she treated me like a close family friend instead of a daughter. We would get a gift delivered on birthdays and Christmas and maybe a phone call once a month. As I was about to slip deeper and deeper into my thoughts, Sandra touched my shoulder. She said, "Sweetie you were a million miles away. I've been trying to get your attention because Chase is here." I smiled at her and said, "I'm sorry, my mind was wandering."

Chase walked over and gave me a hug and said, "Leia, how are you doing?" I mustered up a smile and said, "OK, I guess." Chase asked, "Is there somewhere we can go to talk?"

I told him to follow me, and we went downstairs to the family room. Sandra and Uncle James also came downstairs. I sat down on the coach hoping Chase had the answers to all my questions. Chase stood in front of us and said, "I want you all to know how sorry I am for your loss; it's a loss to me, also. Jason and I go back a long way." We all said, "Thank you."

Chase went on to say, "I want you to know I will personally be working on the murder investigation. I made detective a few months ago, and I will do everything in my power to find Jason's killer. I'll just tell you what we know so far and then if you don't mind, I have a few questions for you guys."

We all shook are heads and Chase went on, "Jason was found in his car at about 2 o'clock in the morning on the Lower East Side. He was shot twice—once at close range—so that leads me to believe he knew his killer. There was a 911 call that was made from Jason's cell at 1:50 a.m. We think it was a man, but we're not sure. Whoever it was whispered, so it's hard to tell. We know it wasn't Jason, because from the pulmonary report from the medical examiner, he died around midnight.

What I can't figure out is why whoever made that 911 call used Jason's cell to make the call, and why he waited almost two hours to call. I also don't think he was killed where he was found; maybe that was the delay in the call." I sat there crying thinking about him being shot and alone, how someone could do that to him, plus to think it was somebody he may have known.

Uncle James stood up and said, "Maybe someone was trying to rob him?" Chase shook his head and said, "I don't think so, James. He still had his wallet and there was $500 still in it and all his credit cards. That's why we ruled out robbery."

Sandra looked at Chase and said, "I just don't understand how someone he knew could do this to him." Chase looked at me and then said, "Mrs. Robertson, Jason was in the game and that can bring some very bad people in your life. Most likely it was someone he trusted. When was the last time either of you saw or spoke to Jason?"

I answered Chase first. "He took me and the kids to dinner at about six o'clock then he dropped us off at home at about eight. He said he would be home before ten. Then I called him at about ten thirty to see when he would be home. He said he was in Minneapolis and was on his way home." I started crying again. I can't believe that the dinner we had would be the last we would have together and that the last time I heard his voice was 10:30 p.m. Chase asked me "When you spoke to him was, he alone?" I answered, "I think so; I didn't hear anyone."

Chase asked, "Sandra did you talk to Jason that day?" Sandra wiped her tears and shook her head and said, "Jason came over about noon. He dropped Oliver off—they were looking at houses we had a late lunch and then we went shopping for Leia's graduation present. He was so happy! I can't believe this one minute I am hanging out with him and having fun and now he's gone!" She put her head down and began to cry. I hugged her because I knew what she was feeling. I missed him, too, and wished this were all a mistake. Then Sandra looked up and faced me with tears running down her face.

"Leia, Jason never got a chance to tell you this, but he had two presents for you. The first I'll give to you after your graduation. The second, I'll tell you now. The reason why Jason was looking at houses was because he was ready to start his business. Jason and Oliver were going to start with one house and after they finished, sell it and buy more. He said he was tired of hustling, and he knew you wanted him to stop. You were done with school this was a perfect time. Isn't it ironic just when he was about to leave the life, he was taken from us?"

I sat there thinking about what Sandra had just told me. Why was this happening to me? Just when he was about to change his life he was killed! I'd prayed every day for him to change, and as soon as God answered, someone took his life! It's so unfair.

Chase walked over to me and Sandra and said, "Thank you both for taking the time to talk with me. Here's my card if you think of anything, will you please let me know?" He gave us his card and hugged us both.

We went upstairs my mother walked over to talk to Chase. I heard him tell her he would talk to her after he spoke with Oliver. Chase and Oliver went in the dining room to talk. My mother was one of Chase's biggest cheerleaders. Chase and I went to the same private school and church and we both came from well-off black families, so my mother wanted us to get together. She never liked Jason; he wasn't the kind of boy she wanted me to date. She didn't know we were dating until she found out I was pregnant.

I went into the day room and sat at the window. I remember when Jason brought me to see this house. I fell in love with it the moment I saw it. Jason wanted to see other houses, but I told him I wanted this one. It had windows in every room and most had window seats. I loved looking out the window and when I told Jason why I liked windows, he bought this house. When I was a little girl Nana would sit by the window in her chair just staring outside. I always wondered what she was looking at, so one day I asked her why she was looking outside. She told me to go into the living room and look out the bay window at the sky and tell her what I saw. I looked out the window and all I saw was birds flying and clouds. She said no, don't look with your eyes but with your heart. I looked again and I felt him. "God," I said. She came over and stood next to me. She looked up at the sky and told me that whenever she was sad or confused or just wanted to feel God, she would sit and look in the sky and feel his glory. And after that, I would do the same and I swear it helped me through a lot of hard times. I was hoping it would help me through this. I buried my head in my knees and cried. I felt someone walk up and I looked up; it was my mother. I really didn't want to deal with her right now and just as I was about to tell her that she started talking.

"Leia, I know how hard this is, but you will get over this." For some reason, all the emotions and anger I felt about Jason's death came out at her. I looked up at her and said, "The same way you got over dad's death?" She moved in front of me and said, "Yes, just like that."

I stood up and looked her in her face and told her what I wanted to tell her for years, "Mother, you didn't get over his death, you just erased him from our lives! You packed up all his things and pictures the day of the funeral, and never said another word about him. How in the hell is that getting over something? You acted like he was nothing to you, like his life didn't matter to you. I only saw you cry one time!" She looked shocked and then she said, "Leia, I was getting on with my life. I was trying to make it easier for you and breaking down wasn't going to bring him back."

I felt the tears coming down my face and I looked at my mother and said, "No, Mother, it wouldn't have brought him back, but it would have showed me you loved him, missed him or hell, that you gave a damn about something other than yourself and your job!"

I could tell that hurt her because her eyes were starting to tear up. She looked at me for a minute and said, "I did love your father, but love doesn't pay the bills and I couldn't afford to shut down. The world doesn't end, Leia. Just because you lose someone doesn't mean you break down and stop living." I shook my head and started to walk away. I stopped and looked back and said, "No, the world didn't end, mother, but your husband's life did!" When I turned back around, Sandra was standing in the doorway and she looked at me and said, "Leia Marie Richardson, don't you dare talk to your mother that way!"

Sandra walked over to me waving her hand as to say I should be ashamed, but the truth was I was ashamed not for saying it, but that Sandra heard me. My mother stormed out. Sandra just looked at me; I turned and walked back over by the window and wept.

Nana came in and sat next to me on the window seat and I laid my head on her shoulder. She said, "Leia, everyone is ready to talk to you." I sighed and told her, "I really just want to take a hot shower and tell the twins so I can go back to bed." Nana kissed me on my forehead and said, "I understand. I'll tell everyone you'll call on them as you need. After I see them out, I'll get the kids from your mother's house."

I took the back stairs because I didn't want to see anyone. I just wanted to shower and wait for the kids to get home. I showered for a while then I just let the water run on me so I could let my mind drift to the last time me and Jason showered together. It was also the last time we had sex. Thursday morning, I was running late and had planned to take a quick shower, but Jason had other plans. He came in, locked the door and got in the shower with me. Just as I was about to tell him the kids were already up and I was running late for their doctor's appointment, he kissed me and pulled me close. I could never, ever say no to sex with him, even if I was mad. Just his touch would get me in the mood, so the kiss was all I needed; nothing else was important at that moment.

He turned me around and rubbed his hands all over my body while he was kissing my neck. I let my head drop back on his shoulder and let out a long sigh. He took his fingers and rubbed them over my nipples getting me hotter and wetter. He turned me around and knelt in front of me and put my leg over his shoulder. When I felt his tongue on me, I fell back against the wall and enjoyed it.

I loved the way he felt inside me, and with each stroke I could feel my-self-getting more and more excited. I stood there, tears running down my face. I screamed, "Why, God, why?" I hit the wall with my hand and slid to the floor screaming and crying.

The shower door opened, and I looked up and it was my mother. She reached out her hand, I took it and she helped me up. She wrapped a towel around me and sat me on my bed. She gave me a kiss on the forehead and walked out. I really didn't know how to feel about that. She hasn't been that caring toward me since daddy died. This was all new, but I am glad she was here.

I didn't want the kids to come home to find me laid out on the shower floor. I dried off and went to the dresser, and instead of going into my drawer, I opened Jason's so that I could get one of his white t-shirts and put it on. I wanted to smell him. He wore Issey Miyaki and no matter what I washed his clothes in, it always smelled like his cologne. As I was finishing getting dressed, I heard the front door close, and a lump formed in my throat. I took a deep breath and went downstairs, and as I was coming down, the twins were on their way up.

I tried to form a smile as I hugged them. I took them to the living room and asked them to sit on the couch, that I had something I needed to tell them. I sat on the coffee table in front of them and looking at their faces, I couldn't help but tear up. I took their hands. I wiped my tears and told them, "There's no other way to say this but to just say it. Your dad died on Friday."

After the words came out, I felt numb, and they both just sat there at first not moving not blinking with blank looks on their faces. The reality must have set in because Lil' Jay started crying and I had to grab him because he was shaking so hard it scared me. As I was holding Lil' Jay, I saw Sandra holding Jada as she cried. We all cried and cried until we had no tears left. Lil' Jay got his thoughts together then asked the question that I really didn't want to answer yet—how Jason had died. I took another deep breath and gave him the answer that would only lead to more questions.

I said, "He was killed, Jay." He looked at me puzzled, like what I had just said didn't make any sense to him. Then he stood up and looked at me and asked yet another question that I didn't want to answer: "How was he killed?" Again, I answered, "He was shot."

He looked confused for a minute, then fell back onto the couch and started screaming and crying. I sat next to him and put his head in my lap. I rubbed his back and told him to let it out, that it was OK. He needed to cry. I knew from what Sandra told me Jason never really cried after his father died. He held it in I didn't want that for Lil' Jay.

Jada came and sat next to me. I put my arm around her and kissed her forehead she looked up at me with tears running down her face. Then Jada asked, "Mom, Daddy's always nice to everyone why would someone hurt him?" I didn't know what to say to her… I wanted to know the same thing. Jason may have been a lot of things, but he was an excellent father. His street life never, ever came home with him. When he was here, he was my husband and their father. He attended all their school functions, he coached Lil' Jay's basketball team. He was there, and that's all they knew and that's all I wanted them to know. I never want them to know about the other life he led. Sandra had left an hour or so earlier; I think the last 45 minutes was all too much for her.

I held the twins until they cried themselves to sleep. My mother helped me lay them on the couch, so they were comfortable, and I sat on the love seat across from them. Looking at their faces, I wondered how I was going to make it through this without losing my mind.

She came and sat next to me and said, "Leia, you have a right to be upset with me. I'm not trying to take that away from you, but I would like to change our relationship. Please let me help you and the kids through this. Please let me be the mother I should have been." I never in my life expected to hear her say that. I looked at her and it was at that moment that I was ashamed of how I had spoken to her earlier.

I took her hand and said, "Mother, all I've wanted is for you to love me and treat me as your daughter, not as some disappointment. I know your dream for me didn't include me getting pregnant at 15 and marrying a drug dealer, but I was still your daughter. Instead of being supportive, you totally abandoned me, but I forgave you for that a long time ago. So, as you're ready to be a part of my life, then yes I'm open to that."

We hugged and I took the twins to my room and put them in my bed. I got in and just laid there thinking about what just happened with my mother. I wanted to think of anything other than Jason. I let my mind drift back to the day mother didn't show up for my performance when I was playing Cinderella. She promised she would be there and when she didn't show up, I was angry. Daddy sat me down on the front step of the school. I was crying, and remember saying, "Daddy, why doesn't she love me?" He wiped my tears and told me, "She does love you baby, but she feels like she has something to prove." I looked at him and asked him, "What does she have to prove, Daddy?"

He took my hand and said, "That she's worthy. When I met your mother, she was working and going to school. Before that life for her wasn't easy, Leia. She was born in Washington D.C. and grew up in one of the worst neighborhoods in the city. As if that wasn't enough, her parents weren't very nice people, and your mother was the youngest of seven kids. They were very poor, and her parents would beat them and there was never enough money for things they needed.

So, your mother started going to the library by her house and she became very close to the librarian. She would allow her to stay there all day even after it was closed. That was her only escape, and she read almost all the books in there.

One day when she was about 17, she met a man at the library, who was older than she was, but he was very nice to her. She thought he was her Prince Charming. He told her that after she graduated, he would marry her and help her go to college. When she graduated, she left home and went to live with him. After she was with Thomas for a few months, things changed drastically. He didn't marry your mother and he had no plans for her to go to college. He became controlling—she wasn't allowed to go anywhere without him, and he started hitting her.

Six months later, she was pregnant with your brother Lance and things got worse. Once Lance was born, she felt trapped, and the beatings got worse and worse. One day she got tired of it and stood up to him and told him that she was going to call the police if he beat her again. For that, he almost took her life. The only good that came from her rebellion was that he let her go, but he wouldn't allow her to take Lance. She moved to Minnesota where the librarian had moved and started college and worked. I met her after she graduated from college and was in law school. We started dating, and I showed her that true love does exist. She's had it bad baby, so don't be so hard on her. Once she makes partner she'll be around more, I promise."

2 CHAPTER

I woke up and looked over at the kids. They were both still sleeping so I headed downstairs to make coffee. Sandra and my mother were both in the kitchen. Sandra was sitting at the table holding a cup of coffee; not drinking it just holding it looking off into space. Mother was busy making breakfast—I didn't even know that she could cook. My mother turned and looked at me smiling and I swear I hadn't seen her smile since my dad died. She was so beautiful! I never noticed that either. I guess I was so busy trying to get her attention that I never really looked at her. With a cheerful voice mother said, "Sit down, I'll get you a cup of coffee." I sat across from Sandra and said to my mother, "Thank you, it sure smells good in here." She sat a cup of coffee in front of me and said, "It should, I've been up cooking since about six."

If I didn't know any better, I'd swear aliens had abducted my mother and cloned her. I looked at Sandra and she was still in the same position that she was in when I first came into the kitchen. I put my hand on her hand and she jumped so hard she spilled her coffee. She didn't say a thing, she just got up and walked out the kitchen. Mother came over to me and put her hand on my shoulder and said, "You better go talk to her, she's been like that all morning. She got here around 6:30 a.m. and that's the same cup of coffee."

I looked up at her and she gave me a grin and went back to her cooking. I got up and went to find Sandra, I was about to go into the living room. I looked down the hall and I saw her sitting on the floor in front of Jason's office. I sat down next to her. She was crying. I took her hand, she was trembling.

She turned and looked at me, and wiping her tears, she looked very serious and said, "Leia, promise me you will never allow Lil' Jay to hustle! Please, promise!" I told her, "Sandra, I would give my life before I would allow Lil' Jay to be in those streets!" She shook her head and said, "I know that you're not like me; I am a horrible mother." I moved closer to her and put my arm around her and told her, "No, you're not, Sandra."

She moved away and said, "Yes, I am. I failed my son. I knew what he was out there doing, but just like with his father I acted like I didn't. I know over the years you've heard bits and pieces about Jason's dad, but I'll tell you everything.

Charles was very handsome and every girl in town wanted him, but none could seem to keep him. I never tried; I just went about my business and one day me and a few co-workers went out on the town. I was sitting at the bar and Charles came in and as usual all the women were around him. He came and stood next to me I didn't even look up and kept sipping my drink.

He looked at me and said "Damn, girl! What do I have to do to get your attention—set myself on fire?" I looked up at him and smiled, and he had me. We dated for about a year and then he proposed, and of course I said yes. My mother was not happy. She knew what he did, and being the good Christian that she was, she didn't approve. Against her wishes, I married him, and I was happy. He treated me like a queen, and I didn't want for anything. It was a few months after Jason was born that I found out about his mistress Brianna Morris. When I confronted him, he didn't lie. Charles would always tell you the truth, no matter what the truth was. He said he had been messing around with her for three years and that he was going to continue to see her. I was so upset I started to pack Jason's and my things, when Charles came in and sat me on the bed.

He asked how knowing about Brianna changed what we had. He also said that Jason and I were his priority, and that would never change. Leia, I don't know why I didn't leave, but I didn't I stayed and accepted it.

What's so ironic is the woman I allowed him to betray me with was the one who took his life. To this day, I still don't know why she killed him. The police believe she was trying to rob him, but I don't believe that. If I would have left, then Jason wouldn't have idealized Charles and he wouldn't have been dealing drugs. See, Charles had a reputation around the neighborhood as being this big shot drug dealer and I think Jason felt like he had to live up to that.

If only I would have talked to Jason and told him that yes, it was Brianna that pulled the trigger, but it was the streets that killed his father. If I had, Jason would be alive today." She held her head in her hands and cried. I pulled her close and held her as she cried. I sat her up and looked at her, tears now running down my face.

I said to her, "Sandra, Jason was a grown man and the choices he made were his, not yours. I guess I was feeling the same way, but hearing you blame yourself for what he was doing makes me realize that it's not our fault. Jason wasn't stupid; he knew how we felt. Yes, we both could have kept talking to him about it, but ultimately it was his choice."

Just then, I looked up and Jada was standing in front of us. She held out her hand, I took hers and Sandra's, and we got up and went into the kitchen.

As soon as we got into the kitchen Jada said, "It smells good in here!" I told her, "I know, your grandmother Lisa made us breakfast!"

We all sat down, and I looked over the spread that mother had laid out for us. There was ham and bacon, eggs, grits, sausage, pancakes and muffins—she even made homemade hash browns. We all grabbed a plate and dug into the food. It was so good that when Lil' Jay came in the kitchen, no one even noticed. He said, "Hey, why didn't anyone wake me up for breakfast?" I got up so I could make his plate I told him, "I am sorry, but you were sleeping so good I didn't want to wake you. Go wash your hands."

Sandra said, "Leia, I asked James if he had spoken to Alicia, and he said you were trying to reach her." I told Sandra, "I had to leave her a message. She's in a remote part of Kenya photographing a tribe and there's no phones so they would have to take her the message. The man said it would take a day to get to her and then another day for her to get back to me. I told them tell her to call her father, and that it was an emergency. I didn't want to say much more; it's bad enough she would have to be told over the phone."

Sandra said, "I know it's going to break her heart. Her and Jason were cousins but acted more like brother and sister." I said, "I know Sandra, this will be really hard for her." Mother said, "You two have always been there for each other and you'll do the same now. You know, Leia, I was always envious of you and Alicia. I never had a best friend."

I smiled at my mother and said, "I know I'm lucky! We've been friends since first grade and if it wasn't for her, I would have never met Jason. I'm twice-blessed that she's, my friend."

Thinking of Alicia makes me sad in a way, because I know that she's going to go crazy when she finds out about Jason. I remember the first day I met Jason. She would talk about him all the time, but in all the years I had known her I hadn't meet him. I was thirteen and he was standing outside the recreation center with Chase and his boys, which was kind of funny because I had a crush on Chase until I met Jason. He was standing there looking good as hell and his smile was what caught my attention.

He stopped us and asked Alicia was she going to introduce him to her friend. "Jason, this is Leia!" she said, waving her hand still walking into the rec like she really didn't want to introduce us. He smiled and said "So this is your best friend? Hello, Leia!" I was smiling and said, "Hi, it's nice to meet you! I've heard so much about you I feel like I already know you." He smiled and said, "Same here!"

As I went inside, I looked back, our eyes met, and I felt an instant connection. From that day on, he would be outside the recreation center every time we went to our homework club Jason would open the door for us. One day he asked me what my favorite flower was. I told him daisies. The next day when we went to the homework club, he was standing there holding a bunch of yellow daisies he sat next to me with his books and to my surprise he was smart, helping me the whole time. He suggested that we exchange numbers just in case I needed his help. I was glad he asked, and we talked every night after that.

I sat there wishing that I hadn't thought about that, because now I was crying and felt like I was going to lose my breakfast. I stood up and headed upstairs. Everyone asked me what was wrong, but I didn't answer. I just went upstairs. I laid on my bed and cried, wishing Jason was here and all this was not happening. But it was happening, and Jason wasn't here.

Jada came in my room, laid on the bed next to me and took my hand. I looked over at her and touched her face. She looked just like Jason. She wiped my tears and we just laid there looking at each other. I stayed in my room the whole day.

Mother kept coming in saying so and so was on the phone, but I didn't want to talk to anyone. When she came and said Nana was on the phone, I even said tell her I'll call her back. About 7:30 p.m. Mother came in and said Chase called. She told him I wasn't up to talking, but she said he wanted to tell me there releasing Jason's body tomorrow. I didn't say anything; I just walked past her and went into the bathroom and started a bath.

I was already so overwhelmed, and now this. I guess it really didn't feel real because I hadn't made any arrangements, but now it was official. I sat in the tub crying and Mother came in and sat on the side of tub, stroking my hair. She said, "Honey, I know how hard this is but I promise you that the things that Jason did that made you smile or all the times you spent together will become precious memories that will make you smile again."

I laid my head back on the tub and said, "I feel like I am drowning." Mother said, "Leia, you may think that it was easy to get over your father's death, but it wasn't. Richard was the only person in my life that really loved me. I cried myself to sleep for weeks until he sent me a sign saying that he was OK, and then the tears stopped, and the memories began."

I looked at her. She had never so much as said my father's name since he died, so this was an amazing moment for me.

I asked, "What sign?" She smiled and I could see all the love she had for him. "You know how your father would spend all day doing his crossword puzzles?" Thinking about that made me smile, because daddy would always have this book of crossword puzzles in his back pocket. I said, "Yeah, he would even do them when he took me to play at the park."

She said, "Well he had a crossword puzzle that he had started the night before he died. He only did three words before I made him turn off the lights and put it in the nightstand drawer. I never went in that drawer; it was your father's and after he died, I really didn't go in it. But one day I was about to get in bed, and I heard this beeping noise. I tracked it down it was coming from your father's drawer. I opened it and it was the alarm on his planner. I picked it up and when I did, I saw the crossword puzzle. It was finished and the first word that I saw was 'peace.' Then I looked over it and the next word I saw was 'heaven' the next was 'everlasting.' Then I knew that it was a sign from your father telling me he was OK! From then on, I was at peace and one day you will be at peace, too."

I was so happy that she told me about that, because up until this point I was convinced that she really didn't love my dad. Now that I am living the same nightmare, I can understand what she was going through. I told her, "I thought that losing daddy was the worst thing that could happen to me, but I guess I was wrong. "

She handed me a towel and I stepped out of the tub and mother said, "Leia, I know I went about it wrong, but you were only 11. I wanted to make it easier for you, so I thought that if we just went on with our lives you would be OK."

I smiled and touched her hand. "I know you tried, Mother. Thank you for being here."

She gave me a kiss on my forehead and left the room. I knew she was trying to help, but she kind of made it worse. Now not only I am thinking about Jason, but now I'm thinking about dad. I guess it would have been easier if they both had been ill, but they weren't. In each case, they were ripped from us.

Daddy was killed in a head-on crash during one of Minnesota's worst winters. I will never forget that day. I would always go to Nana's after school and daddy would pick me up a few hours later. I knew what time he usually came, so when it was 4:30 p.m., I was looking out the window and he wasn't there. I asked Nana why he wasn't there, and she said it was snowing hard so he might be a little late. I waited and half hour and went back to looking and he still wasn't coming. It wasn't until about 6:00 p.m. that I could tell Nana was getting worried. She called his office and a few other places.

Then at 6:45 p.m., my mother called I answered the phone. I could tell something was wrong by her tone. She just said, "Give your grandmother the phone." I gave the phone to Nana and after a few seconds I saw her smile turn into a look of horror. She told me to go into the living room. I sat on the couch and wondered what was going on. I knew it was bad because I could hear Nana crying. Then Aunt Jackie came (she was Nana's sister and my cousin Nate's grandmother), and she rushed into the kitchen and closed the door behind her. I sat there wishing daddy would come—he would know what to do. It was about two hours later when mother came, she walked in and came right to me. She sat on one side and Nana sat on the other. Nana wrapped her arm around my shoulder and mother took my hand. She looked at me and told me that my dad wouldn't be coming home anymore; that he had been in a car accident, and he didn't survive. That was the first time I felt real heartbreak. I didn't think I would ever feel safe or secure again until I met Jason. Now here I am again feeling the same as I felt when I was 11…scared and unsure of how I was going to get through this.

The two things that absolutely stopped me from losing my mind were my kids and that my mother is here, but I needed Nana. She was the only person who could seem to make any situation bearable. I dialed Nana's number and then I looked at the clock. Shit, it's 10:00 p.m. I just knew she would be asleep.

I let the phone ring three times and I was about to hang up when I heard Nana's voice say, "Leia, are you OK?" I asked, "How did you know it was me?" She said, "Lucky guess." Before she could get another word out, I started sobbing. I was trying not to cry, but I was in so much pain. Nana said, "Leia, I am on my way O.K., baby?" Then the phone went dead.

This felt like déjà vu. I was 15 again calling Nana, telling her that mother was putting me out. Just like now, Nana came running. She was the first person I had told that I was pregnant. I was so ashamed and scared, I practiced what I would say, and then thought about what her reaction would be. Each time was worse than the last, so I just did it. I walked to her house thinking, "I'll just say it and accept whatever her reaction was. By the time I got to the first step of her porch, I lost my nerve. I was about to turn and run when she came out on the porch.

Nana said, "Well, that was a quick visit!" I stopped. My first thought was to run, but I didn't. I just stood there not wanting to turn around. I had promised myself I wasn't going to cry, but the tears were rolling down my face

Nana came down the stairs and said, "Leia, whatever is on your mind, we can figure it out together." I slowly turned around by now it looked like I had sprung a leak.

She grabbed me and hugged me and said, "What's wrong? Tell me what's on your heart." I went and sat on the step and put my face in my hands and started sobbing. She took my hands down from my face. She said, "Now, look at me and tell me what's wrong." I took a deep breath and looked at her and told her that I was pregnant. To my surprise, she said she already knew that. She said, "I've known you all your life. I knew when you were sick before your mother or father. I knew when you needed a hug after a bad day at school so there isn't much you can get past me!" I felt so low I put my hands on my face and began to cry, and again she took my hands down.

She wiped my tears and said, "There is no use in you beating yourself up; what's done is done. Now you must decide what you're going to be." I looked at her, confused. "Are you going to be one of those girls who gets pregnant young and does nothing with your life, or are you going to be the young woman you were raised you to be? You can do anything you set your mind to, and I'll be there every step of the way." I looked at her and I was so thankful that I had Nana. She was more than a grandmother—she was my rock.

I told her, "I'm sorry Nana. I never thought this could happen. Please forgive me."

She smiled and said, "Leia, it isn't for me to forgive you because I love you and there is nothing you can do to make me stop loving you. But you need to ask God to forgive you." I told Nana, "I am going to do everything in my power to give this baby the same life as I have. And I will finish school and go to college." She hugged me and said, "That's what I want to hear, but God help you when you tell your mother, because it's going to take a miracle for her not to kill you."

I sat there thinking of how I was going to tell my mother, and the real outcome wasn't far from what I had imagined. I got off the bed and went and looked out the window, not thinking, just looking at the stars. I heard the door downstairs open and close. I knew it was Nana, and when I got downstairs. She was sitting on the couch I went and sat next to her. She put her arms around me and said, "Baby, it's all right. I am here!" Before she could get the rest out, I started crying. I looked up at her and just like back then, just her being here made me feel much better.

I said, "Nana, this hurts so much sometimes it hurts to breathe! What will I do without him?" She rubbed my hair from my face and looked me in the eyes and said, "Live. I know it's hard to lose someone you've spent most of your life loving. When your grandfather passed away, I felt the same emotions you're feeling right now. Your father became the reason I got up every day and each day it got a little easier to get up. God knows our pain and he knows how to help us heal from that pain. Pull strength from God and trust that he will give you what you need to make it through this."

I laid my head on her lap and before I knew it, I was asleep. When I woke up, I was on the couch, and it was morning. I went in the kitchen, and Nana and mother were already up. I walked in and kissed Nana on the forehead and said good morning. As I was about to sit down, Nana hit my side. I knew what she was trying to say so I went to the other side of the table and kissed mother on her forehead and sat down. Nana made it a point to tell me that mother took a leave of absence from work so that she could be here. I didn't want to act surprised, but I was. Mother had worked hard to become partner at her law firm, the only woman to make partner and the first black lawyer at her firm. I don't think she's ever taken a day off or even a vacation, so I must admit I'm shocked.

I smiled and took her hand and said, "Thank you, Mother. Your being here is a big help." She looked at me with tears in her eyes. "I am putting my family first from now on. That's the way it always should've been. I can't change that now; Lord knows if I could I really would." I went and gave her a hug, not because I felt she needed one, but because I waited my whole life to hear her say I was important to her.

I excused myself and went upstairs. I had to hurry today. It was the day I had dreaded, because Sandra and I had to meet with Howard. He was doing Jason's funeral (he owned Wilkins Funeral Home and plus I knew Jason and Howard were cool) and Howard's son and Lil' Jay are best friends, so we see a lot of each other. I went and got in the shower not thinking I didn't want to think—I just wanted to make it through the day.

I got dressed, went downstairs said goodbye to Mother and Nana, and got in the car. It wasn't until I was in front of Sandra's house that it all hit me. There wasn't anything I could do, the tears just kept on rolling down my face. I kept telling myself, "Get it together, girl!" but that wasn't helping. So, I just got out and went to the door, hoping that I would stop before Sandra answered. By the time she got to the door, I managed to pull it together. She didn't even look at me. She closed the door and headed for the car. I understood why and let it go. We didn't talk or play music, we just drove. When we got there, Sandra looked over at me and said whatever I wanted to do was fine with her. I could make all the decisions.

But there was something strange going on with her. I couldn't put my finger on it, but it was just something in her demeanor. I hadn't been at Wilkins Funeral Home since Daddy died and it looked totally different. When Howard's dad owned it, it was such a sad-looking place. But now the waiting room had warm inviting colors and Yolanda Adams was playing in the background. There were nice couches and chairs and magazines with people smiling on them. We sat on the couch and what really made me know that something was wrong with Sandra was that she sat far away from me. Just as I was about to ask her what was wrong, Jasmine came over and sat down next to me and said, "Howard and I are sorry about Jay. How is Lil' Jay taking it?" I replied, "Thank you. He's handling it as well as to be expected, but he'll be all right with time."

Just then Howard came over and took my hand. Without him even saying anything, I knew what he was trying to say. Sandra and I followed him in his office, and we sat down. Still, Sandra hadn't said a word, even when Howard gave her his condolences. Howard handed me this folder it had Jason's name on it and said, "I knew this would be hard for you, so I took care of everything. Look it over and see if it's OK." I opened it and he had chosen the top of the line for everything, and as he had said, it was all done, and I approved. I tried to hand it to Sandra to look over, but she declined. I looked at her and she still wouldn't make any eye contact, so I said, "Howard, everything is fine, but I do have something that I want done. I want him buried in a navy-blue Armani suit with his platinum cuff links, a fresh cut and I want him to be buried with his wedding band." Jason always looked good even when he was on the grind, so that's how I wanted him to look at the visitation and the funeral.

Howard said, "That's fine, I'll pick up the suit for you." I told him, "Jason has life insurance so everything will be covered," and then gave him the insurance papers. He took them and said, "I'll handle everything, and you'll definitely get a huge discount. I owe Jay, so this will clear our debt." I said, "Thank you; call me if you need me to do anything." Howard stood up and took my hand and said, "You're welcome and you both have my number. Don't hesitate to use it."

I was so glad to get out of there I really wanted to talk to Sandra she seemed distant when we got in the car and I asked, "Sandra is everything all right?" She replied without even looking at me, "Yes, I am fine. I really need to get home."

I knew something was wrong, she didn't want to I talk about it. I didn't want to push, so I dropped it, even when she got out the car without saying goodbye. I was so emotionally drained. I really didn't want to go home; I wanted to feel safe, so I went to the one place that made me feel better. Daddy would always take me to the park by our house and I would play for hours. I sat on the bench watching the kids laugh and play I longed to be that happy again. I started thinking of daddy pushing me on the swing—he loved pushing me and he would make me go so high! I would always say, "I want to touch the sky, Daddy!" and he would reply, "I can't get you that high, but I'll get you close!" Just then another memory popped up. This time there was a woman standing on the side laughing, telling daddy to stop or I'd be sick. Once I was done, she took my hand and we walked to the grass and had a picnic. Just as fast as the memory came on, it went away. I sat there trying to bring it back, but it wouldn't come back to me.

I decided to go home. The whole way, that woman's face was planted in my mind. As I was pulling up, I saw Lance's car in the driveway.

Shit, I really didn't want to be bothered with his ass. He's my half-brother, but we've never really been close. He really wasn't around much, because his father would make mother pay him to allow Lance to come visit, and daddy wasn't having that.

It wasn't until daddy died that Lance really started coming around. I am sorry—he's my brother, but his presence makes the hair on the back of my neck stand up. When mother was at work, it would be just Lance and me. He wouldn't say a word to me, he just stared at me. Plus, one day I woke up and he was standing over me just looking at me. After that, I would make sure I would be up and ready when mother left so I could go to Alicia's or Nana's house. Nana would always say if you wanted to see what someone was made of, just look in their eyes—a person's eyes are the windows to their soul. I did that one day with Lance, and I swear I saw pure evil! From then on, I limited my dealings with him.

I walked in and everyone was in the family room. I sat down next to Nana, and Jada and Jason both came over and kissed me. Lil' Jay was so much like his father; so caring and thoughtful. He asked me, "Mom, are you feeling, OK? Do you need anything?" I smiled at him and replied "Yes, would you bring me some tea and those pills on my nightstand?" As he walked away, he asked, "Anything else I can do?" I replied, "That will be all, thank you baby"

I wanted to go upstairs and go to sleep, but I felt the need to ask about the woman in my memory. I wasn't sure if it even happened even though it seemed real. Mother put her hand on my knee and asked, "How did it go at Wilkins?" I told her, "Fine. Howard took care of everything before we got there. I just had a few things that I wanted done my way." She replied, "That's good—it takes a lot of the pressure off."

I told them how Sandra was acting and that I was worried about her. I also told them that she didn't talk at all and didn't want to have any input on the arrangements." Nana reassured me. "Leia, I know what it's like to lose a son. She just needs time; she'll be OK." I looked at Nana and said, "I hope so Nana, I really do"

Then I told them that after I dropped Sandra off, I went to the Dowling Park so I could think. I had a memory, or at least I think it was a memory. Nana smiled and said, "Child, you and your daddy spent hours at that park. I think he enjoyed it more than you!"

I smiled too and said, "I know, Nana that's why when I am down, I go there. I can always see dad there, but in this memory, we weren't there alone. There was this woman with us standing by the swings while daddy was pushing me." Nana replied, "Maybe she was one of the other parents. Your daddy and you were there so much everyone knew you guys." I said, "No, Nana, I think she was with us."

I left out the part about the picnic. I wasn't sure what this memory was about, but I did know that there was a woman there and she was with daddy and I, so I wanted to be discreet.

Mother interjected, "Leia, it's like Nana said. It was probably another parent; so, can we drop it?" I could tell by the look on her face that she knew who I was talking about, but she didn't want to say. Like I did with Sandra, I let it go.

After that we all sat there for a moment with this awkward silence, then mother broke it and told the kids to go upstairs and get ready for bed. They both left and mother followed. It was just me, Nana and Lance left. Nana took my cup and said she would get me some more tea. I wanted to say no—I didn't want to be left alone with Lance—but I just gave her this look and I guess she didn't know what that meant because off to the kitchen she went. I was about to get up when Lance started talking.

"So, you had a memory of your perfect father cheating on mom?" He laughed I wanted to get up and slap him in his face. How dare he say anything about my dad! Instead, I said, "Lance, this is none of your business, so keep your comments to yourself!" He laughed again and said, "No, I just think it's funny that her knight in shining armor betrayed her!"

Now I was truly irritated, so I said, "Let's keep it real... your dad makes Ike Turner look like a saint. The next time you want to comment on my father, please look at that animal that you call your dad!" He didn't say anything at first; he just looked like he was going to explode.

Then Lance said, "You know you're so sad, you really are. You sit here in this nice big house with all these nice things like you're better than everyone. When the fact is your husband was a maggot feeding on the lowlifes of the world and your dad was a two-timing loser. So, don't look down on me and my father. We work hard for what we want, not peddling drugs!"

I chuckled and said, "Are you serious? You're really a joke! Work for it? Yeah right, is that why your dad would make mother pay him one thousand dollars each time you came to visit? Yeah, that's what a good parent does, so please don't go there," I was fuming. "Plus, when Jason was alive all, you did was kiss his ass. But let me make myself crystal clear: if you ever disrespect my husband or my father again, you'll regret it!"

I was about to get up and walk away when he jumped in my face. I thought he was going to hit me, but Nana came in the room and yelled, "What in the world is going on?" I guess from the yelling and the fact that we were face-to-face and neither of us turned she could tell it was drama. I didn't back down. I stood toe-to-toe with his ass shaking not because I was scared, but I wanted him to hit me so I could have Nate beat his ass.

Nana came over and stood in front of me and said, "Boy, you better get out of her face and sit down!" He stepped back and Mother came in looking confused and said, "What's going on? I heard yelling!" Nana turned and looked at her and said, "I was trying to figure that one out myself. You hear your mother, Leia Maria?" I said, "Her bastard son started talking about my dad and my husband!

Nana said, "Leia Maria Richardson, now I know you're upset, but you better mind your manners!" I was sorry for cursing in front of them, but he had no right to say the things he said.

My mother took Lance's arm and walked him into the hallway, and he turned and said "Oh yeah, I forgot. She's a princess."

I walked behind them, and I told my mother, "No, I am sorry mother if you want to talk to Lance you'll have to do so from the porch, because he is no longer welcome in my house." She looked at me and said, "Leia, he's your brother and you don't do that to family. Whatever the problem is we'll work it out together."

I looked at her and said, "Mother, that's your son and I'm sorry but I don't want him in my house." I walked out and went to my room. In a way I was glad this happened so now I didn't have to see his scary face again. I looked out the window with tears rolling down my face. I missed

Jason so much. I was standing there thinking how life will never be the same how alone I felt.

Lil' Jay came in my room and stood next to me and asked, "Mom, are you all, right? I heard you and Uncle Lance yelling." I hoped he didn't hear everything, plus I didn't mean to snap while the kids were around. But I couldn't let Lance disrespect my family. I told him everything was fine, but he informed me that he called my cousin Nate. I gave him a hug and assured him everything was all right and sent him to bed.

I called Nate; he was about five blocks away and hyped up. I told him that Lance left and that I would call him tomorrow and tell him all about it, but I didn't want to go through it tonight. I hung up and went and got my sleeping pills and got in the bed.

As soon as I started to drift off, the phone rang. All I heard was sobbing. I said, "Hello, who is this?" and then I heard the person say, "Leia, I am so sorry I really want you to know that!" I realized it was Tee.

I said, "Tee, where are you? I've been trying to get in touch with you for days!" She replied, "That's not important. I need you to forgive me—please tell me you forgive me? "I was confused but said, "OK, Tee, I forgive you. Now tell me where you are I'll send someone for you."

She quickly said "No, I'm OK. I just want you to know no matter what, I love you and the kids and if I could change things I would. Leia, there are some things that I will never be able to take back but know if I could, please don't hate me, please! You have always been like a sister to me, and I want you to know that!" Then the phone went dead. I kept trying to call her cell, but she wouldn't answer so I gave up.

I knew Nate was in the streets, so I called him and told him to look out for Tee. He wasn't too happy about that because he didn't like her, but he said yes for me. I said a prayer for her so that God could watch over her and help her through her grief. Besides Jason and me, Tee didn't have any other friends. She did have a whole bunch of women who would fall head over heels over her, but she dismissed them as fast as she got them. I waited for a while to see if Nate or Tee were going to call but they didn't, so I rolled over and let the sleeping pill take effect.

3 CHAPTER

I woke up to the phone ringing. I looked at the clock it was 7:00 a.m. I rolled over and decided to let someone else get it. I really didn't want to talk to anyone right now. Nana came in and rubbed my arm and she whispered, "It's Alicia." I sat up and I felt and instant knot in my stomach, picked up the phone and said hello. Alicia asked, "Leia, are you OK?"

Trying to fight back the tears I replied, "No, Alicia it feels like someone has ripped out my heart!" At that moment the tears I was fighting won we both just sat on the phone and cried. After a while, Alicia said, "You know Leia, this is fucking crazy, I talked to Jason last week! I called to tell him I was coming to your graduation party. He was so happy he told me he was going to stop hustling, Leia, why?" I wished I could give her an answer but that was the same question I was asking.

She started crying and I just listened. I knew she needed to get it out and I was so glad she was. Alicia always kept her feelings to herself until she couldn't anymore and then she usually blew up. After a while I could hear the phone breaking up. Alicia told me it was a 17-hour flight and that she was leaving soon and going to stay with me and the kids.

I hung up and got up and went downstairs when I walked by the day room, I saw Lil' Jay sitting in his dad's chair looking at a picture. I went and sat next to him, put my arm around him and asked, "Do you want to talk about it, baby?" He looked up at me and said, "Mom, was dad killed because he was dealing drugs?" I sat there caught totally off guard by what he had asked. How in the world did he know what Jason was doing and how do I answer his question?

Before I could say a word, he said "Mom, before you answer, please tell me the truth. One day at church when I was having an argument with Tommy Wilson, he said at least his dad wasn't going to hell. I said my dad wasn't going to hell either, then he said yes dad was because he was a drug dealer. I asked dad and he told me he did things that he wasn't proud of, but I didn't need to worry about that. All I needed to worry about is being the intelligent, self-confident young man that you guys are raising me to be."

I was so angry those gossiping ladies at that church! Always in someone else's business! They all smile in your face but talk mess behind your back. I took a deep breath and said, "Jay, I want you to know that your dad may have been doing things that he shouldn't have been doing, but he was a good man."

Jay looked at me and said, "I know that, Mom. Me and dad talked for a long time about it I just gave you the short version. I understand, I just want to know why someone would kill him." I felt just as lost as Jay did, but I told him, "Jay, at this point I don't know why someone killed him and once we find out who, then I think the why will be next. I pray Chase will find the person soon so we can have closure." Jay gave me a big hug and went to get some breakfast. I didn't feel like eating, so I sat there stunned by our conversation. I'm glad Jason talked to Jay because at least he'll know that his father would never want him out in the streets selling drugs.

I decided to go sit on the bench in the middle of the garden I go there almost every day. It's a place where I can go to have my me-time with God. I planted roses directly across from the bench, so when I sit there the roses are the first thing I see. I sat down and looked at my rose bushes and to my surprise they were already in bloom, which was odd because they usually didn't bloom until early June. I closed my eyes and just smelled the fresh morning air, hoping it would somehow cleanse me of my pain. I felt a nice breeze wash over my face and when I opened my eyes there was a single rose petal on the bench next to me. I looked down and picked it up then I looked at my rose bush. There was one rose fully bloomed and tears rolled down my face. I put my head in my hands and cried and then felt another cool breeze. This time when I opened my eyes, the whole rose bush had bloomed. I went over to the rose bush and felt and smelled the roses. Thinking to myself that maybe I'm still asleep, but it did happen...I just couldn't figure out how it happened.

Nana came out and said everyone was leaving to go to church. I was glad she didn't ask me to go; I really didn't want to look at those ladies today. Tomorrow was the visitation, so today I just wanted to rest. I went inside to make myself something to eat, when the doorbell rang, I was surprised to see it was Chase. He said he didn't have any news for me, he just wanted the check up on me to make sure I was doing OK. I thanked him and asked him to come in and we went into the living room and sat down.

Chase said, "I wish there was something I could say, Leia, to make this easier for you. I remember when we were kids at church, Pastor Williams would always say, "Knowing and loving God doesn't mean that we won't go through strife, loss or heartbreak, but knowing, loving and having faith in God will always help us out of it." I looked at him and I started to cry; I needed to hear that.

He asked about the kids, and I told him they were doing as well as could be expected, but with a lot of love and support they'll be OK. Chase said, "I am sure they will be. I couldn't imagine being their age and losing one of my parents. It's good you have lots of people to help you." I smiled and said, "I know; I am truly blessed to have a great family."

Chase cleared his throat and said, "Leia, I don't want to make a hard time harder, but I heard something, and I wanted you to know." I took a deep breath and thought for a minute before I asked him what he was talking about, because at that point I couldn't handle much more. I reluctantly said, "What did you hear, Chase?" He looked at me and said, "My mother ran into Sandra's friend at the grocery store, and she said that Sandra somehow blames you for Jason's death."

I sat there for a moment and then I said, "What? That's ridiculous! I don't believe that; Sandra and I are close, and she would never say or think anything like that!" Chase replied, "You're probably right, I just wanted you to know what was said. Well, I've got to go. I'll see you tomorrow."

He took my hand and held it and I had a flash back that I have tried to forget. I never thought about what happened between me and

Chase—I blocked that night out of my mind. Aunt Sheila and Alicia were the only two people that knew that I had cheated on Jason with Chase. It was the biggest mistake of my life. Jason was sleeping with this girl who lived by his mother's house; I found out when he didn't come home one night. I had called him about a hundred times, and he didn't answer I was so worried I went to Sandra's house. As I was going down Sandra's Street, I saw Jason's truck parked outside this woman's house who lived a few houses away from his mother. I went to the door and when she opened it, you'd thought she saw a ghost. She didn't say a word and I'm glad because my intention was to kick both their asses. Jason came to the door trying to explain and I slapped the shit out of him and ran and got in my car and pulled off. I ended up at this bar downtown drinking and crying. I was on my sixth or seventh drink when Chase came from nowhere and sat down. He tried to take me home, but I told him I didn't want to go home, not yet. I told him to take me to a hotel, but he said no he would take me to his house and make me coffee and then take me home. When we got there all I can remember is we were talking and somehow, we started kissing and sex followed.

When I woke up a few hours later I got up got dressed and took a cab to Alicia's. Even though she was Jason's cousin, I knew she would be there for me. I told her what happened, and she wasn't mad; she said that's what Jason got for fucking that hood rat. We both decided to let it go and to never bring it up again and that's just what I did. I wasn't up for bad memories, so I decided to go to the gym and try to work out some of the emotions I was feeling. Just as I was pulling out of the driveway, Nate was pulling in. I told him I was going to the gym, and he got in. We drove to the gym and after I pulled in and parked, he had this look on his face and I knew he had something to say.

I looked over at him and said, "What's on your mind?" He looked at me and from that look I knew it was drama. Nate always worked but he also hustled from time to time. If anyone in the family knew, he would probably get his butt handed to him from everyone. We were cousins, but we were more like brother and sister. Since his father wasn't around and daddy wanted a son, he treated Nate like his son. We spent a lot of time together and after dad passed, Nate felt he had to be my protector. Nate shook his head and said "Man, that stupid-ass brother of yours is going to make me hurt his ass!"

I quickly asked, "What did he do now?" He went on to say that after we hung up the other night he went by this bar where he knew Lance would be. When Lance saw him, he told the bouncer that Nate was harassing him. That sounds like Lance's scary ass. I chuckled and told Nate, "Just leave it alone please for me. Just squash it, OK?" I gave him this sad look so he would agree. I didn't want him to hurt Lance. Believe me, I wasn't thinking about Lance, I was concerned for Nate. I didn't want him to end up in jail and plus my mother would be hurt if something happened to Lance. He looked at me and then he grinned and said, "All right, Cuz, only because you asked, but this is his only free pass. The next time, that ass is mine!"

We went in the gym, and I worked out while Nate tried to pick up women. I think I sweated more in this workout than any other. By the time I was done, Nate had found him a victim so I left him there because he said he would have her drop him off at my house. I laughed and made my way home. They still weren't back from church, so I decided to shower and find something to eat.

As I was on my way upstairs, I saw the message light blinking on the answering machine. I wanted to ignore it, but it might be a message from Alicia. She was due home sometime today or tomorrow. It was Sandra and she said, "Leia, I won't be riding with you to the visitation or the funeral. Please have my grandkids give me a call," and then a click. At first, I really didn't believe what Chase said, but I think there might be something to it. Sandra has been acting really strange the last few days. I know she's hurting so maybe she just needs her space; I sure hope that's the case.

I got in the shower and when I got out, Jada was sitting on my bed looking sad. I sat next to her a put my arm around her and asked her what was wrong. Jada said, "Mom, I'm scared to go see daddy." I told Jada that tomorrow would be one of the hardest days of her young life, and that I was going to be by her side the whole time. Then I got dressed and I spent the rest of the day with the twins, and we talked about what would happen tomorrow. I wanted them to have an idea of what to expect, even though I knew that it was going to be hard on all of us.

I got up the next morning and the whole house was up and getting ready. Nana was like a drill sergeant, so the kids were already dressed and having breakfast. All I had to do was get myself together, which took me an hour or so. I know Nana was surprised because it usually took me longer, but today wasn't a day that I wanted to be running behind.

We were to arrive at the visitation at eleven o'clock so that family would have an hour to view the body alone. It didn't dawn on me until now that we would have to take Jason's truck because we all weren't going to fit in my car. I never drove his truck (it was too big), so I would drive my car or his Cadillac. We piled in and I smiled because the truck smelled just like him. I was adjusting the seat and flipped down the visor and he had our family picture taped on it. I touched his face and smiled.

We drove to the wake listening to a gospel CD that Nana put in. In one of the songs the woman said, "This life may not last long, but heaven was always" and for the rest of the way there I kept saying that in my head.

We pulled up to the funeral home and I felt sick to my stomach. I took a deep breath and got out the truck. I kept telling myself to be strong because the kids needed me, so that I would keep it together.

When we got inside, Sandra and the rest of her family were already inside. When we walked in, everyone came to our side except Sandra. They were hugging us and telling us it would be all right. We sat in front with the twins on opposites sides of me and I told them they could view his body when they were ready. I stood up and as I was about to go view Jason's body, Sandra was walking down the aisle toward me. I stood in front of her and held out my hands she just pushed past me and walked toward Pastor Williams. I was about to go after her, but Nana took my arm and said, "Go visit with your husband."

I turned and made my way to the casket and looked down at him and I swear he had a smirk on his face. So instead of crying, I smiled and touched his face. The twins were both in tears and came and stood beside me. I held them close, and we just stood there looking at him, wishing he wasn't laying there. But he was, so all I could do was hold my babies and tell them their dad was with God now. We stayed for an hour and then we left. I didn't want to be there while other people viewed his body; I just couldn't handle that. The twins cried so much they were sleep by the time we made it home we got them out the truck and put them in their beds.

I went out to the garden and looked all the roses were in bloomed, and right in the middle of my red rose bush was one pink rose. I smiled and looked up and told Jason thank you. I knew this was his way of helping me through this. I smiled and sat there just looking at the roses. As I was walking up to the house I looked up in the sky and there was one cloud over our house. In my heart, I knew that was Jason looking over his family, so I went inside and went to take a nap. When I woke up and looked over at the window, Alicia was standing at the window looking out. I got up and went over to her I put my hand on her shoulder. When she looked up at me, tears were running down her face and she said, "What are we going to do without him?" I looked at her and shook my head we stood there looking out the window and crying.

After a while Nana came in and said that Alicia's dad was here. I was glad he was, because we didn't get a chance to talk at the funeral home. Alicia run up and hugged Uncle James so hard I thought he was going to fall over. Then he came over and hugged me. James took my hand and said, "Leia, I heard how Sandra acted. Don't mind her, she's just mourning. She'll be all right, just give her some time."

After he said that, it hit me that Chase was right—Sandra was blaming me. I started to cry, and James held me and said, "Leia, sometimes grief can make people do or say things that they don't mean. Give her some time. After my brother died, she didn't want to see anyone and that only lasted a week. She'll be all right—she just needs to find a way to deal with this." I hoped so, because we needed her, and the kids had been asking why she hadn't been by.

When James went home, I took Alicia up to the second guest room/my office. It used to be the attic, but Jason turned it into an office for me. It was so big that I put a couch in there that folded out to be a full-sized bed and put a TV, a dresser, plus a huge desk. Alicia looked around and smiled then said, "It's beautiful up here! Did Jason do this all by himself?" I smiled and said "Yes, he worked on it every day, Girl! He was going to make money with his business—he was good at remodeling." We both sat on the bed and cried. This time I was crying because Jason had so many talents and it was sad that they were wasted.

I left so she could get some sleep I went and laid across my bed and before I knew it, I fell asleep with all my clothes on. I woke up about 6:00 a.m. and went downstairs. Nana and mother were both already up moving around the house getting it ready for the guests after the funeral. The company I had hired to set up the tent and the chairs and tables had already come and went. The food was already arriving; I had three different soul food restaurants catering. Nana and mother wanted to cook, but I said no there was going to be a lot of people and I didn't want them to be cooking for days.

I wanted it to be in the house but the food to be served outside. Jason loved having dinner parties in the yard; it was huge, and we spent a lot of time on the landscaping. He loved showing off his work, that's another reason I wanted it to be outside. I went outside to make sure it was set up as I had requested, and it was. I was about to check the tables when mother came over to me and said, "You go inside and get the twins ready. We have everything under control." I looked at her and gave her a kiss on the check and said, "Thank you, Mom. I hope you know how glad I am you're here." She smiled the biggest smile I had ever seen and took my hands. With tears in her eyes, she said, Thank you!"

I went in the house and got the twins up so they could eat and start getting ready. The limos would be here at nine o'clock. We all got ready and at nine on the dot, the two limos were out in front. James and his wife were already here, and Jason's half-brothers were also here. Sandra and her husband weren't there yet, so we called Sandra's house. We got no answer, so we waited fifteen minutes then we just left.

The whole way to the church I kept thinking about Sandra and why she would make this my fault. She went from blaming herself to blaming me I heard someone say once that death was ugly, but the way some people acted after someone died was even uglier. I guess that is very true because I would have never guessed in a million years that this would be happening. We finally arrived and I saw Sandra's car in front of the church. I took a deep breath and made my way inside. Jason's little cousins were the ushers and they walked us to the front of the church, and we sat in the front pew.

I looked around to see that Sandra was sitting up front, but she was in the pew across from us. I wanted to go to her, but because we waited for her, we were just in time for the service. Reverend Williams started the service by quoting some verses from the Bible and then talked a little about how precious life was and how we should treat every day as if it were our last. Then he looked at me and the kids and said, "I prayed over you and Jason the day you two started your lives together as man and wife, and now I will pray over Jason's Journey home. I know that someone took Jason from you, but no one will be able to take the memories that you shared. Find peace in knowing that Jason is with God, and he will always be with you. Love and mourn him but not for too long, for he is OK because God took him home."

I sat there as tears fell from my eyes and instead of being sad, I felt at peace because I did know that he was with God, and that no matter what Jason would always be by our side. After he said a few words to Sandra then to the twins, it was time for people to speak about Jason. The first person who was supposed to speak was James, but he was too broken up to speak so Alicia got up there and talked on behalf of both me and Uncle James. Then Lil' Jay got up and spoke about his dad how he was always there for him. As he went on, the cries in the church were like a choir.

I had asked Jada if she wanted to speak, but I knew that she wouldn't want to. She's a very emotional person and she wouldn't have gotten one word out. One by one, people got up and spoke, and then it was time to say our final goodbyes.

I let Sandra go first and then I went up and looked down at him and with tears running down I spoke to him. "I've loved you from the first time I met you. You were my husband, my best friend and the father of my children. Basically, you were my whole world. I will miss you and you will always be in my heart and mind."

I gave him a kiss and stood back so that the twins could have some time to say what was on their hearts. As they carried out his casket, my cousin Anna sang, "His Eye is on the Sparrow" the whole church was in tears. We followed the casket and I stopped at the door because I wanted to talk to Sandra before we left for the graveyard. When she walked past, I took her hand and pulled her aside. I asked her, "Sandra, what is going on?" She looked at me with disgust and tried to walk away, so I took her hand again and said, "Sandra, at the very least you owe me an explanation." She snatched her hand away and said, "I don't owe you anything, Leia, but you owe me a lot!" I stepped back and gave her this look and then she said, "Jason had to sell drugs because you up and got yourself pregnant!" Before she could finish, Chase stepped in between us and took me by the arm and said, "Leia, it's time to go. The police escorts are ready."

He walked me to the limo, and I was crying so hard I couldn't even talk. Alicia thanked Chase and helped me into the limo. I cried the whole way to the graveyard, because what she said really hurt me. She knew that my getting pregnant wasn't something I planned! Why would she say that? Also, Jason was already selling drugs back then; he was supplying all the kids in the neighborhood with weed. Alicia tried to comfort me, but I was so hurt and angry there wasn't anything she could say to make things better. When we got to the grave site, I was a mess, but I slowly got out and made my way to the plot. Pastor Williams said a few more words and my cousin Anna sang, "Precious Lord, Take My Hand" by Mahalia Jackson while we put roses on the casket as it was lowered into the ground.

As I was walking back to the limo, Sandra came up to me and informed me that she would be by tomorrow to get Jason's things which included his clothes, the contents off his office and his truck. I took a deep breath and asked God to help me remain calm. I told her, "Sandra, I told you, you're more than welcome to come get some of Jason's things, but you aren't going to take everything."

She started yelling and said, "Jason always felt like he had to do more because of who your family was and that cost him his life. You have the insurance money, now you want to keep everything?" I was about to let her have it, but Alicia stepped in front of me and said, "Sandra how dare you blame Leia for what Jason was doing? You and I both know Jason was selling drugs long before he and Leia met."

Then Sandra went on talking about how I trapped Jason and because of that he had to continue selling drugs to support me and the twins. The funny thing was she didn't even know her own son. I told Jason I could stay at Nana's until I graduated and finished college. Between Nana and me, and my trust, we would be fine. Jason wasn't having it—he said he was a man, and he would take care of his family. Before I could reply to her craziness, James took Sandra by the arm and pulled her away.

I wanted to slap her; I really did. I looked up and told Jason I was sorry, but I would never ever speak to his mother again and she wouldn't be around our kids. I was so glad I didn't let the twins come to the graveyard, because it would have really hurt them to hear Sandra say the things she said.

Alicia took me to the limo gave me a big hug and we went to the house by the time we got there everyone was there. After what happened at the grave site, I really didn't want to see anyone, but I had to. I told myself that I just had to get through this. Sandra didn't come and I was glad, because I don't think I would have been able to keep myself from slapping her. To avoid all the people, Alicia and I went up to my room. I needed and few minutes to gather my thoughts.

We sat on the bed and Alicia said, "Leia, Sandra was really out of line, Girl. I was trying so hard not to cuss her ass out!" I looked at her and said, "I'm glad you didn't. She's your aunt and that would have been wrong, even though I had to bite my tongue a few times. "She looked at me and said "Girl, please! She's my cousin's mom and you know me and her really weren't close, because she called herself not liking my mom."

I told Alicia I was so hurt because Sandra was always like second mother to me. To have her say the things she said really broke my heart. Alicia gave me this look and said, "Sandra has always been a little off'. I asked her, "Why do you say that?" She smirked and said, "What woman in her right mind would allow their husband to lay up with some other women? Girl, please, she takes down-ass chic to a whole different level."

I giggled and said, "Amen, I have to agree; I really don't understand why she went for that." Then Alicia said, "Girl, they say love is

72

blind, but hell it must be crazy and half insane to make a woman let that type of thing happen." For the first time in days, Alicia managed to make me laugh because we were cracking up.

Nana came in and gave me a look as if to say why aren't you downstairs, so we got up and made our way to the kitchen. As soon as I got down the stairs, I saw Sandra walking through the back door, and I stood there for a minute. I really was amazed that she had the nerve to show up after how she acted. Nana walked over to Sandra and used a tone I seldom heard her use and said, "Sandra, don't you come in here with no mess, because the last one you made hasn't been cleaned up." She gave her this don't-mess-with-her look and walked out.

Sandra walked past me and went and sat with the kids. Alicia looked at me, rolled her eyes and went outside. I felt trapped. I didn't want to go outside and have everyone asking how I am and all that stuff, but I didn't want to be in the same house with her. I went outside and Chase must have been reading my mind, because every time someone would linger to long Chase would step in. Then it was finally over. People were making their way out and I was so happy. I was glad that James and Chase stayed to help clean up.

I was so tired physically and mentally that I went upstairs and got in the bed. I fell asleep as soon as my head hit the pillow, and I swear morning came too fast. I was dreaming about the day I finished my garden. The kids were at Sandra's and Jason was gone so I planned a nice picnic for myself. I was sitting there eating my fruit and admiring my work when Jason came home. He came out with his hands behind his back. "What are you hiding?"

He knelt and kissed me on my forehead and handed me some roses without saying a word. He sat next to me and started rubbing his hands through my hair and kissed me. I loved kissing him; his lips where so soft and each kiss was filled with so much passion. He laid me back on the blanket and started undressing me. He took a rose petal and rubbed it across my body and kissed each part the petal touched. Then he licked from my navel to my lips and my whole body felt like I was on fire. He was so gentle when we made love.

It started raining but we didn't stop. We were so caught up in our lovemaking that I didn't care that it was raining until we were done, and by then it was pouring. I sat up and a tear fell from my eye. I would never feel him that way again. I got up and went downstairs. I needed to feel close to him, so I went to his office. I stood at the door for a moment and took a deep breath and went in. His office was nice. He set it up a few years ago, he said he was getting it ready for his business. I sat in his chair and looked around for a few hours, not touching anything, just sitting there. My mother came in and stood beside the chair and stroked my hair, not saying anything just trying to let me know she cared. It felt so good, and I really felt close to her. It's a shame it took for me to lose my husband to gain back my mother. Nana came in and she smiled. She's always wanted mother and I to be close; she said it was unnatural for a mother and daughter not be close.

Nana came and stood in front of the desk and said, "Leia, my sister Mae Lynn had a stroke a few days ago, she needs a lot of help and Ray can't handle it alone. Those sorry children of theirs won't be much help. So, I am going down there to help her out and I was thinking I could take the twins. I think it would help them right now to get away and you know they love going down south."

I didn't want them to leave me right now, but Nana was right— they loved going to Alabama. Aunt Mae had a big, beautiful house and land as far as the eye could see. Plus, I know they really do need to get away. It would be good for them, so I said yes. I went to the family room to tell the twins and when I did, they both jumped up and down with joy. But I told them they would have to help Nana and Uncle Ray with Aunt Mae and they both said they would. I was kind of sad because Nana said she was leaving day after tomorrow, so I only have a day to process them leaving for the summer. They've never been away from me that long and after losing Jason I don't know how I was going to feel with them gone. I told them I would take them shopping to prepare them for the trip and that made Jada happy. I left the twins in the family room, because I wanted to touch base with Chase in private. I really hadn't talked to him about the case, and I wanted to stay on top of it. So, I went in the living room so I could call him.

Chase said he didn't have any new information, but as soon as he had any new information, I would be the first to know. I hung up feeling very unsatisfied; it's already been a week and he still didn't have any leads or a suspect. I knew from watching all those detective shows that the first few days are critical to solving a murder.

I got up and went back into Jason's office, but this time I was looking for clues. I thought that maybe there was something here that could lead to who and why Jason was killed. I went to the desk, opened the front drawer and the normal stuff like pens, paper clips and change was there. I looked at the first drawer on the left, tried it and it was locked—so were the other drawers. I went and got his keychain but none of the keys fit...damn, where would he keep the keys?

I started thinking about the last time I found something Jason had hidden from me. I went to the family room and looked behind the chest but no luck, so I sat in the chair and thought about where I had seen him around the house the last few weeks. Got it! I came home and I found him in the garden a few times. He was kneeling by the water fountain, and I remember I joked that he was finally praying.

I went in the garden and looked at the fountain. It looked normal, so I felt under the bowl and jackpot! The keys were taped to the bottom of it. Now I was curious as to what was in the drawers that would make Jason lock them and hide the keys. Jason knew I didn't go in the office when he wasn't home, and the twins also knew that was off limits.

I went back in the office, closed the door, sat down in the chair and opened the first drawer. In it was a notepad that had pages of letters, then behind it numbers and then dollar signs and amounts. I figured out this was his way of keeping track of who he dealt with, what he gave them and how much he got from them and how much they owed. I looked it over and to date no one owed him money, so I set that aside to burn. I knew Jason would want me to get rid of this, so I would do what I thought he would want me to.

The next thing I saw was another cell phone—that was weird because to my knowledge he only had one. I turned it on and went through the phone book. Nothing popped out, so I went to the messages. There were six coded messages, so I assumed that this was the phone he used for business. Finding the phone put a new spin on his death, because if the phone he used for business was here, then it didn't have anything to do with his hustling.

I put the phone on the "get rid of" pile then I looked at some other papers that were his investment portfolio. I set that aside so that I could call his broker. Then the rest was just the normal car repair bills and other paperwork, so I moved to the next drawer.

Now that's when things got interesting. There was a big brown envelope and in it was a notebook, some handwritten notes and the transcripts of the trial for the women that killed his father. The notebook pages were in Jason's handwriting and the first page was a list with Allen Thompson (Chase's dad) at the top. The next was Peter Wilson and then Brianna, the woman that killed his father. By each name, he had written comments. By Allen's name, it said, "number one suspect" and after Peter's, it said, "witness or accomplice," and after Brianna it said "innocent." I sat back in the chair my mind was swirling. Jason was looking into his dad's murder and the hard part was how was I going to tell Chase about all of this. Hell, his father was who Jason thought did it!

I read every page of his notebook. He had written down random thoughts, along with some facts that he had gathered, including times and places as if he was following someone. I closed the notebook and put it all back in the envelope and locked it back up and put the keys in my pocket. I took the pile of things I was going to dispose of and went to do just that.

I was in such a fog that I was standing in front of the fire pit trying to make sense of what I had found. After I started the fire, I threw all the stuff into it. As I watched it burn, Alicia came out of nowhere and scared the hell out of me. She looked at me and said, "Girl, isn't it a tad bit too warm for a fire?"

I told her, "I was in Jason's office, and I found some things that blew my mind. I didn't think Jason's death had anything to do with his drug dealing. The phone he used was locked in his drawer so that meant he wasn't on business that night. Second, I found a notebook that leads me to believe that Jason was looking into his dad's murder."

She looked shocked and said, "Leia, why would he be doing that? Brianna was convicted of killing my uncle so why was he looking into his death?" I told her I had no idea why Jason was looking into his dad's murder, but the only thing I knew for sure was that I needed to think about it for a while to decide what my next move was going to be. I knew one thing for sure: Chase wasn't going to like the fact that his dad was Jason's prime suspect.

I decided all this was too much to deal with right now, so I took the twins shopping. When we got to the mall, I gave them each one hundred dollars and told them to stay together and meet me back at the main door in an hour. Since they turned thirteen, they informed Jason and I that they were too old for us to shop for them, so Jason and I talked it over and realized that they were right, and they needed to feel independent. I went to a discount store in the mall to get them socks and underwear and lots of tanks because it got hot as hell in Alabama. I got the things I needed and made my way to the check out and I ran into Tee's ex Stacy. She was a nice, beautiful girl and was the smartest girl in our school. I hated her because she always beat me out in a few academic awards; I was always a score behind her in every test. Her ass even beat me out for valedictorian. So, it surprised me when Tee brought Stacy over. Tee was attractive, but she treated the girls she went out with like they were nothing. She wasn't faithful and they gave her money. I was surprised Stacy stayed with Tee so long. I would always ask Jason how Stacy could put up with Tee's mess for five years. Tee dogged Stacy out… she cheated on her and didn't hide it at all I always thought Stacy deserved better.

Stacy walked over and said, "Leia, I'm so sorry about Jason, girl! I've been a mess since I found out. I saw you at the funeral, but I didn't want to be a bother—I know how it feels to lose someone that you love." I smiled and said, "Thank you." She told me that her mother passed away a few months ago, and I said, "Oh my goodness, I didn't know! I'm so sorry for your loss." She thanked me and said,

"It must be hard. If you ever need to talk or just want to hang out, I'll give you, my number. By the way, how is Tee doing? I noticed that she wasn't at the funeral, and I've been calling her and stopping by her place, and I haven't been able to catch up with her."

I replied, "I wish I knew how she was doing. I haven't talked to her or seen her, and I was surprised she didn't come to the funeral, I replied to be truthful, I'm really worried about her. It's not like her not to call me." She told me when I did get ahold of Tee to have her call her, and I assured her I would.

As she walked away, all I could think was she still cares for Tee after all she put her through... she must have a heart of gold. I made my way home, packed the twins' bags and went to sleep. When I woke up, I took the twins and Nana to the airport. I hugged the kids so tight I didn't want to let them go. I said I wasn't going to cry, because I didn't want them to be sad. I waited until they boarded the plane then the flood gates opened. I watched the plane take off and I headed home.

On my way, I called my cousin Nate and asked him to meet me at the house. He was reluctant because he knew Alicia was staying with me, but I told him it would be fine. But I knew that Alicia wouldn't be happy Nate was coming over. They had dated for years and when Alicia got pregnant, unlike me she didn't keep the baby. Nate was angry when she told him she wanted an abortion; he wanted the baby, but Alicia had always planned to go to NYU, and she said she didn't want to give up her dream. She had the abortion and what really tripped me out about the whole thing was that Alicia had the nerve to be mad that Nate wouldn't go to the clinic with her. Ever since, there has been tension between the two—Jason and I even had to have someone keep them apart at our wedding.

I pulled up and went inside Alicia was on the deck I went out and sat across from her and said, "Alicia, I know what I am about to say is going to sound crazy, but please listen first, OK?" She gave me the here-we-go look and said, "OK, I am glad I have a drink because it sounds like I am going to need it." I said, "Well, I've been calling Chase and he still doesn't have any leads. If he doesn't find some soon, we might never know who killed Jason and I was thinking we could try to find answers ourselves. All we have to do is prove that Jason's theory was right or wrong."

She took a sip of her drink and said, "Leia, you're right, I do think it's crazy. But I also know that Jason is just another dead black man to the police. Chase knows as well as we do that, they're not going to give him the resources to get this solved. So as crazy as your idea is, count me in because Jason needs justice!"

I jumped up and gave her a big hug and then I told her the other news that I knew she wasn't going to like. "I know you're not going to be happy about this, but I'm going to ask Nate to help. I put my hand up to stop her from talking and went on to say, "Before you say anything, he's the only one I could ask that would actually help us." She quickly said, "Fine, but keep him away from me!"

Alicia got up and went in the house, and I leaned back in the chair wondering if this was the right thing to do. The door opened and I heard Nate, so I went inside so I could avoid a scene between the two of them. As I was making my way to the kitchen, Alicia was walking back out on the deck mouthing, "Keep him away from me!" I shook my head and went in the living room.

Nate kissed me on the cheek and sat on the couch and said, "Hey, Baby Girl!" He was smiling so hard I had to ask, "Why are you smiling?" He chuckled and said, "I love how every time her silly ass sees me her whole day is fucked up." I shook my head and told him he was being petty. Nate responded "No, I'm not. She killed my baby, so this is her punishment."

I wanted to change the subject. I understood both their sides of this issue, but I had to say "Nate, look. I know that she hurt you, but you need to forgive her and let it go. Really, it's been years and you two are adults, so please find a way to get along with one another." Nate said, "Leia, you may not think so, but I have forgiven Alicia. She's the one that's torturing herself—I just take pleasure from that!" I shook my head, smiled and let it go. I went on to tell him the reason I called him over.

" The reason I wanted to talk to you I was going through Jason's desk and discovered that he was looking into his father's death. For some reason, he didn't believe that Breanna was the real killer; he thought it was Allen Thompson. I was thinking that he must have found the evidence that Allen was the real killer and that's why he was killed. I wanted to ask you if you'll help me, and Alicia look into this?"

Nate sat back and looked at me for a few minutes and said, "Leia, you know I would do anything for you, so if you really want to do this, count me in. Did you tell Chase about what you found?" I replied, "No, I didn't, and I don't plan to until I have the evidence that points to Allen or someone else as the killer."

Nate sat up and said, "Leia, I think it would be helpful for him to know, because he could use the resources, he has to help us." I knew that, but I also knew that this news would be hard for Chase to hear, so I told Nate for now we won't tell Chase. Nate reluctantly agreed then asked, "Where do we start?"

I replied, "I'm going to start with Breanna. I plan to find out as much about her as I can from Jason's notebook. He thought that she was covering for Allen, and I plan to find out if that was the truth. I want you to find out as much as you can about Allen and since Sandra's not talking to me, Alicia will try to find out as much as she knows about both."

After Nate left, I told Alicia what I wanted her to do and then went into the family room and got on the computer. I figured that I would be able to find some information about Breanna Morris. I started with a name search, and it listed two Breanna Morris's, one in St. Paul and one in Memphis so I clicked on the one in St. Paul. I had to pay to get more information, so I put in my credit card number and a lot of information popped up. She was born in Baton Rouge, Louisiana and it listed her mother as Clara Birmingham, but no father's name. It listed a phone number for her and that was all I needed.

I got off the computer and called Chase. I wanted to see if he had any information, plus I asked him to see if he could locate Tee. He said he was on his was out of the office and he had some stops to make, but he could meet me somewhere. I suggested we meet at Wong's, my favorite Chinese restaurant. It was 7:30 p.m. and I knew there would be a long wait time for a table. I got there and it was packed—they have the best egg rolls in the city. I sat in the waiting area and who do I see but Jewel? Jewel was the best friend of the bitch that Jason had cheated with. I was really hoping she didn't say anything to me, but no she wanted to be messy. When she stood in front of me, I gave her this why-in-the-fuck-would-you-think-it-was-OK-for-you-to- talk-to-me look and she kept it moving. I didn't like having hate in my heart, but those hoes are two people I hate. They go around sleeping with everyone's man or husband and then have the nerve to act like they're all that. A hoe is a hoe; I don't care how you dress it up. I was so glad when I saw Chase! We had to wait 30 minutes, but at least I had someone to talk to.

I told Chase, "I am so glad you came when you did. I thought I was going to have to act ghetto in here!" He laughed and looked at me the way he did when we were kids when I would get mad at those stuck-up girls at our private school we went to. Chase said, "Now who's ass do I need to kick up in here?" We laughed. I swear he will never change—that was the same thing he would say in school. I replied, "You didn't see Jewel sitting over there with her latest victim?" He looked across the room and then laughed as he spotted them and said, "Poor guy, he doesn't know what he's got on his hands!"

He sat back and whispered, "I've always wanted to ask how you found out Jason was messing with ole girl." I looked at him and said, "Long story, and just thinking about it makes me mad, so let's talk about something else." He quickly changed the subject. "Well, I haven't had any luck locating Tee. Have you heard from her?" I shook my head and told him, "No, I haven't, but I brought her spare key. I was wondering if you would go over there with me?"

Chase agreed to go with me to Tee's house, then he told me he had made some progress. A trucker that was dropping off a load 30 minutes before Jason was killed said he saw Jason's car and there were two men in it. He also said there was a car parked in front of Jason's car; he didn't get the whole license plate, but he remembered two numbers "32." Chase said, "That helps for two reasons: first, it proves Jason had to know his killer and second, it's a longshot but all I have to do is find that second car."

I told Chase, "You're right, finding a license plate off two numbers is a longshot." Then he went on to say that it really wasn't, because all he had to do is look in the database, find a drug dealer that has 32 in their license plate, and he'll have a suspect. I reluctantly said, "Chase, Jason wasn't dealing that night, so that won't lead you to his killer."

He looked at me with a puzzled look and asked, "How do you know Jason wasn't dealing that night?" I took a breath and said, "I went through his desk and his cell that he used was in there. Also, Jason had his wallet on him, and I know for a fact when he was on the grind, he never took his wallet with him. He would leave it on the nightstand." Chase looked at me with this look which meant he wasn't happy. He asked, "Leia, why didn't you call me and tell me this when you found this out? It really would have been helpful. Where is the cell now? I would like to have it; it might be helpful to the case." I know he was really going to be upset but I had to tell him, I said, "I'm sorry Chase, but I destroyed it. There wasn't anything that would be helpful to his murder."

Chase replied, "How would you know that Leia? Look, I know why you did that, but you've known me since preschool, and you should know that I would never betray you or Jason! So, whatever was on that phone would have been between me, you and Jason" I touched his arm and looked at him and said, "Chase, I know that, but I thought it was in the best interest of all parties that it should've been destroyed."

I could tell by the look on his face he was hurt. He felt as if I didn't trust him, and in a way, he was right. I knew at one time he always had my back, and I also knew that he did his share of hustling back in the day. But now he was Chase the Detective and to be honest, it's been years since I'd seen him, so I did what I felt was right. I hoped he would understand that I couldn't take the chance.

Chase was quiet through the rest of dinner. When we were done, we got in our own cars, and he followed me to Tee's house. I don't know why I was so scared to unlock the door, but I was. Once we got inside everything looked fine, so Chase decided to look through her drawers to see what he could find. I headed over to her desk because I knew she kept something like an appointment book and was hoping that it was still there. When I opened the drawer, instead of her appointment book there was an ultrasound picture. I picked it up and looked at it on the top right corner it said twelve weeks and on the top left corner it had Tee's real name, Tanisha Johnson. I sat there trying to process Tee being pregnant I must have had a blank look on my face because Chase took my arm and asked if I was all right. I handed him the picture and sat back in the chair by the look on his face I could tell he was just as shocked as I was.

Chase looked at me and said, "This has got to be a joke." I shook my head and replied, "No, Chase, I have twins this is a real ultrasound!"

After that we were both in shock, so we put the ultrasound picture back where we found it and left. The whole way home all I could think about was oh my God, Tee's pregnant. When I got home, I was hoping that Alicia was home so I could tell her about Tee, but unfortunately, she wasn't there. I had to try to put this whole thing together by myself. Tee wasn't just a lesbian she was butch. I remember asking her once if she ever thought about having kids and she said once she found the right woman she would settle down and would take the necessary steps for her partner to get pregnant.

4 CHAPTER NAME

I woke up to the sound of Luther Vandross playing and thought, "Good, Alicia's up!" I jumped up like a little kid on Christmas and went down to the living room. Damn, she wasn't there or in the kitchen. I heard something in the basement, so I went down, and Alicia and her dad were down there putting some boxes in one of the storage rooms. Uncle James came right over to me and gave me a big hug.

He asked how I was doing, and I told him I was hanging in there. I asked him how he was, and he answered, "Better. I'll never be the same, but I'm trying to get through this. I know you and the kids need me." I replied, "We sure do!" We hugged again and this time we cried while we held one another. I think we both needed to cry for each other. I wanted to lighten up the room, I said, "I have some tea that is going to blow you two away"

Alicia always knew when I had some juicy gossip, she said "Girl, let it out you look like you're going to bust." I blurted out, "Alicia, Tee is 12 weeks pregnant!" Alicia looked at me with this hell no face and said, "What? You must have lost your damn mind! Tee pregnant? That's crazy!" Uncle James gave Alicia this no-you-didn't-just-curse look. She quickly said, "Sorry, Daddy, but really?" I laughed and said, "No, it's true she's pregnant. It caught me off guard as well!" We went upstairs and I dropped it because I knew how James felt about Tee. The way he was acting made me think he didn't want to hear about it.

I decided that today I would look for Tee not only because I was worried, but now I was feeling a little uneasy about her absence. I understood that she might need her space for the first few days, but now that I know she's pregnant I really needed to find her, because she might be putting her unborn child in danger. Tee had a bad habit of drinking and doing lines of blow and I wanted to make sure she was OK.

She was seeing this stripper named Lacey who lived on the East Side, so I went over there. I thought she would be home since she danced at night, but she wasn't home. I waited for fifteen minutes but I decided that I would have Nate go to the club and talk to her tonight. My next stop was back to Tee's. There had to be something I missed, plus I was really hoping to find her there.

When I got inside, I could tell she had been there. The ultrasound picture was gone, and it looked like she took some clothes. Just as I was about to look around, the phone rang. I started to answer it, but I let the machine get it. It was Lacey calling to see if Tee was still here. Then she said she would meet her at the spot and that she should bring her the cash. Why was Tee hiding and who was she hiding from?

I looked around I found another notebook that had Tee's handwriting in it. It was like a log where she was following a few people. I could tell because there were initials and arrival times, leaving times and names of places. Some of the initials I could figure out, like "A.T." was Allen Thompson, "B.M." was Breanna Morris, but I had no idea who "J.P." and "C.L." were. Then I saw she had written whether it was her or Jason who was following each person. Now I really had to find Tee! She was running and I needed to know who she was running from.

I called Nate and Alicia and told them both to meet me at Hottie, the club where Lacey worked. It was early, but maybe that's where her and Tee were meeting. I waited outside until I saw Nate pulling up and Alicia came a few minutes later. I showed them the notebook and I told them about the message that Lacey had left.

Nate said, "Leia, we need to find her. I think you're right. Jason's death most likely has something to do with his father's death." I replied, "I know, Nate, and this proves it. Tee's running from someone and we need to find her so she can tell us who that someone is."

We sat there waiting the bartender said that Lacey's shift started at 7:30 p.m. It was only 6:30 p.m., so we had an hour to wait. Instead of waiting in there, we went to the diner across the street where we could see who was coming in and out. Nate thought waiting inside wasn't a good idea because Tee might see our cars and not come in, so we parked around the corner and walked to the diner. It was a very uncomfortable wait because I was so worried about Tee and her baby. I hoped we would see her.

It was about 7:15 p.m. when we saw Lacey pull up. She got out and went inside and we waited until 8:15 p.m. before when went over there. We didn't see Tee come in, so we decided to go talk to Lacey. I went up to Lacey while she was giving a lap dance and I told her to come to our table when she was done.

She came over with this grin on her face. "Leia, this is the last place I would expect to see you!" I said to her, "I'm here to see if you know where Tee is." I could tell from the look she gave that she knew but wasn't going to tell me. Then Lacey said, "You need to drop some cash, or my boss will be over here trippin." Nate gave her a twenty.

She started dancing in front of Nate and he waved her my way. "She's asking the questions." She looked my way and smiled and said, "It would be my pleasure." Even though I didn't want her shaking her ass in my face, I guess Nate was right: I did need to talk to her.

I asked her, "When was the last time you talked to Tee?" She spun around and grabbed my knees and started dancing. I was uncomfortable and I could tell she knew it, but she continued. She replied, "I think about a week ago." I looked at her and said, "I think it was more recent than that." She looked at me and smiled and turned around and started grinding my leg with her ass. I really wanted to get up, but I had to find Tee. Lacey said with a smile, "What makes you think it was more recent?" I said in a matter-of-fact voice, "Let's just say I know it was sometime today." She turned and looked at me puzzled and quickly said, "It wasn't, and sorry, your time's up." Nate pulled out another twenty, but she walked away. Alicia went after her, but Lacey went to the bar and told the bartender something and a bouncer came over and took Alicia by the arm. Nate ran over there and told him to get his hands off her.

The bouncer let go of Alicia and said, "You three need to leave now!" Instead of making a scene, we walked out. I asked Nate, "How am I going to get her to talk to me?" Alicia said "Leia, it seems she has a thing for you, I think it would be better if you went by yourself." I looked at Alicia and from her smile I knew she was enjoying this, so I said, "Don't play with me. Alicia. She was doing her job."

Then Nate deicide to also pick at me. "Leia, Alicia's right. Lacey was having a lot of fun trying to turn you out." I laughed and said, "Fuck you both, but if it will help find Tee I'll go talk to her tonight after she gets off." As Alicia was getting in her car she yelled to me, "Don't do anything I wouldn't do!"

Nate and Alicia went back to my house, and I went to Uncle Joe and Aunt Joan's. They lived on the East Side, plus Nate said they were mad that I hadn't been by. I pulled up and my uncle was sitting on the porch talking to his neighbor. I went and kissed him on the forehead and went in the house. Auntie was in the kitchen putting away some cake.

They were my great aunt and uncle, but we were very close. Auntie said, "Looks like you're just in time to have some cake!" I sat at the table almost foaming at the mouth—she was the best cook, and her cakes and pies were to die for. My dad would always say, "I told your auntie she could give Sara Lee a run for her money!"

Auntie said, "How have you been holding up baby?" I told her, "I'm taking it one day at a time Auntie." She replied, "That's good. So have you talked to Nana since she's been in Selma?" I told her no, I was going to call her and the kids tomorrow.

Then I asked her, "Auntie, do you know who Breanna Morris is?" She stopped cutting the cake and looked at me with this strange look. And said, "Yeah, why?" I said, "I was just asking. You know she was the one who killed Jason's father." After that she continued cutting the cake and put it on a plate. I wondered why she acted like that when I asked about Breanna. She sat the cake in front of me and said, "Who didn't know her? That heifer had every black man in town trying to get at her."

I asked Auntie, "Did you ever talk to her?"

She said "No, but you know my friend Emma? Her sister Pam is Breanna's best friend, and she goes and visits Breanna every week." I was going to ask her for Emma's number, but I didn't want her to ask me too many questions. I knew that Emma worked at the community center off Selby so I would just call there and get Pam's number.

I wanted to get all the information Auntie had, so I told her I never knew that, and she said, "Yeah, Emma doesn't like it, but Pam has been friends with Breanna ever since she came to Minnesota."

I stayed at my aunt and uncle's until almost midnight and then went and sat outside Lacey's house and waited for her to come home. Four hours later, I saw her pulling into her garage and I saw Tee's truck inside. When she got out the car and saw me, she smiled and waved me inside the house. She turned on the lights and told me to have a seat because she had to change. When she appeared again, she had on some tiny sleep shorts and a tank.

She asked, "Would you like something to drink?" I said, "No, thank you" She smiled and said, "I hope you're here to see what comes after the dance... "I quickly said, "No, that's not why I'm here I need to know where Tee is." She sat down and looked at me and said, "Leia, look I know what happened to Jason and I'm so sorry for your loss, but I can't tell you that."

I went and sat next to her and said, "Look, I know your trying to protect her, but you don't need to protect her from me. That's one of the reasons I want to find her, so that I can help her." She looked like she was thinking about what I had just said, then she got up and pulled a bag of weed out of her purse and started rolling it. And said, "Leia, look, I swore to her I wouldn't tell anyone where she was."

I pleaded with her, "Lacey, I know why she's running, and I can help her if you tell me where she is. I know you don't want to break her trust, but Lacey, I need to find her before Jason's killer finds her." She looked up at me and she looked surprised that I knew why Tee was running. She lit the joint and hit it a few times and passed it to me. I stopped smoking weed when I was 20 and I really shouldn't have, but with all that was going on I needed it. I hit it a few times and passed it back to her. I swear you don't know how much you miss something until you do it again.

Lacey told me she rented Tee a hotel room in Duluth, and she was going there tomorrow to take her some money. I asked her if we could both go together, and she said, "Fine, be here by 10:00 a.m." I thanked her and left.

When I got home, I saw Chase's car parked in front of the house. I went in and he was sitting on the couch and soon as I came in Alicia noticed right away. She said, "Leia Marie Richardson, are you high?" I smiled. I really don't know why, but I couldn't help it. Then Alicia came and looked in my face like she was my mama and said, "Your ass is high, me and you will be talking after Chase leaves!" Then she went upstairs waving her finger my way.

Chase asked, "I thought you gave weed up." I said, "I did, but with everything going on I needed a distraction." Then Chase said, "The reason I came by was to see if you found anything else that would help in my investigation?" I hated lying but I did. "No." Chase looked at me for a minute, then he came and sat next to me and asked me again.

I replied, "What? I said no." Chase looked at me and said, "Leia, you're not a good liar so what else did you find?" I stood up and walked to the kitchen. I was feeling a little flushed and I didn't know if it was the weed or the lie, but I needed a drink. Chase followed me in the kitchen. I poured a glass of wine and sat at the table. Chase sat across from me and gave me this look like he wasn't backing down, so I might as well spill it.

Chase said "Look, Leia. Jason was at the top of the game, so whoever killed him probably wanted to be the top dog. Plus, if this person thinks you have some information you might be in danger." I quickly said, "Well, thank you for your concern, but I don't think I'm in any danger. I don't think Jason's death had anything at all to do with his lifestyle." Now Chase was looking at me like he knew I was keeping something from him and said, "Now why are you so sure of that, Leia?" I took a deep breath so I could think a minute, but my thoughts weren't very clear the weed really had me on blank mode, so I did something that I hoped I wouldn't regret. I said "Look, I found this notebook in Jason's things, and it showed that he was looking into the death of his father. I believe he found the real killer and that's why he was killed."

Chase sat back in his chair and said "Leia, Breanne Morris was tried and convicted of the murder of Charles Richardson, so how could there be another killer?" I asked him, "Have you ever read the transcripts of the trial?" He responded, "No, I had no reason to." I told him, "Well, I did and there were a lot of holes in the prosecution's case. Plus, Jason didn't believe she did it and I don't either."

He stood up and started walking around and grabbing his chine then he turned and look at me with this I can't believe you kind of look. He asked "Leia, do you have any idea what you're saying?"

I shook my head and said "Yes, I do...that Jason was killed because he found his dad's real killer." Chase sat down and said "Let's just say you're right about all this and there is a connection between Jason's death and his dad's death. How I'm I supposed to prove this? Also, when did you plan to tell me this?"

I decided to fill Chase in. "Nate, Alicia and I are looking into it and when we have a suspect, you'll be the first to know." Chase looked at me then he sat back in his chair and said, "Are you out of your mind? If what your saying is true, this person has already killed twice! What in the world would he do to you if you start nosing around? What you're doing is unsafe, so I'm telling you to stop. I'll investigate this. Give me the notebook and anything else you have, and I'll do the detective work."

I sat back in my chair and looked a Chase and told him, "I can't do that." I really couldn't give him the notebook or the other information I have, because his father was the main suspect. Chase stood up and looked down at me and said, "Leia, you have lost your mind. Look, you can trust me and it's fucking bothering me that you don't. I've always looked out for you and always had your best interest in heart, like when I found out the narcotic unit was planning to watch Jason, I told him so he wouldn't get caught up. I did that for you and the kids! I knew you needed him, so stop treating my like I'm out to get you!" I stood up and took his hand and said,

"I am sorry, Chase. I do trust you, but there are other reasons why I can't give the notebook to you. Please just believe me that if I could, I would." He just stood there and looked at me for a moment then he sat down looking very frustrated.

He took a deep breath and said, "Leia, I am not leaving until you give me the information and promise me that you'll stop this detective shit or give me a damn good reason why you can't." He folded his hands and sat back in the chair. I knew he wasn't playing, but I had to call his bluff. I started walking out the kitchen and I looked back and said to Chase, "Well, I'll get you a blanket because I'm about to shower and take my behind to bed."

He got up and followed me and said, "Cool, I'll see you in the morning." I looked at him puzzled and I could tell he was serious. I grabbed a blanket and gave him a pillow and went upstairs. I was sure once I got out the shower he would be gone. I needed him to be gone. I was meeting up with Lacey tomorrow and I didn't want Chase tagging along.

When I got out of the shower and went downstairs, Chase was still here knocked out, shoes in front of the couch and his pants and shirt folded over the arm of the couch. He was wrapped up in the blanket. I had to smile; he was still pig-headed I remember that was just how he got his first kiss from me. He posted up in my tree house and wouldn't leave until I gave him a kiss his crazy ass stayed in that tree house for almost eight hours. I got so frustrated because I wanted to play in there with my dolls, so I gave him a kiss just to get rid of him. I looked at him again and shook my head, turned off the lights and went to bed.

5 CHAPTER

I was awakened by Alicia jumping in my bed almost on top of me.

I sat up and looked at her and she had this weird smile all over her face. I

asked her, "What in the hell is wrong with you?' She said with this silly grin,

"Girl, Chase is down there on the couch with a muscle t-shirt on and some

boxers and his friend is pointing north! Back then I didn't want details, but

girl looking at him now that brother is packing so I am going to need some

details now!" I looked at her like she was crazy and laughed... I couldn't

believe her! I tried so hard to block that night out of my mind and now she

wants me to revisit it.

I said, "I thought we swore to never bring that up again?" Still

grinning, she said, "Yes, we did, but things are different now. Jason will

never know, and you know that was the only reason we made that pact, so

girl you're going to have to tell me something!" I looked at her and she was

dead serious. Then she said, "OK, then just answer this: was it good?"

I smiled and said, "OK, fine—it was more than good...now let's leave it alone. Plus, I didn't get a chance to tell you that Lacey knows where Tee is and she said she'll take us there today at 10:00 a.m., so we need to get rid of Chase. She got off the bed and headed for the door and looked back at me with a smile and said, "I'll leave that to you!" I got up and went downstairs and he was still asleep, and his friend was still pointing north. Looking at him brought back all the memories I had suppressed. I touched my neck and said, "Damn!" then I heard Chase's voice. "Damn, what?" Even though he asked the question, I think he knew because he was smiling, and he looked down at his friend then at me and stretched which made me want a cold shower. As I walked in the kitchen I said, "Oh nothing, I was just thinking out loud." I heard him say, "Really, what were you thinking about?" I yelled back "Has anyone told you: that you ask too many questions?" He laughed and said, "Never!"

When Chase came into the kitchen, I was making coffee and he sat at the table. I grabbed two cups and stood there until the coffee was done brewing. I didn't want to turn around until I had control over my thoughts. I made me a cup and I poured orange juice in the second cup and put it in front of him and sat down. Chase looked at me and said, "So, are you ready to give me what I want?" I looked at him for a moment and thought we're not eight anymore and this standoff would be won by me. I responded,

"Chase, like I told you last night, I have my reasons for not giving you the information. I wish you would just trust that and leave it alone."

Then Chase said, "I can't, because if what you said last night is true, that could help me find Jason's killer. I am sorry Leia, but you're going to give me the notebook, so stop being so stubborn and just give it to me."

Just as I was about to reply, my cell phone rang, and I ran in living room and grabbed it out of my purse. It was Lacey. She was crying and screaming and the only thing I could make out was the name of a motel in Duluth, then she screamed, "Hurry, hurry!" and then hung up. I didn't have time to process what she had said, I just turned to Chase and told him. "Look, we'll have to talk about this later. We need to get to Miller Point Motel now."

I made my way upstairs and went to tell Alicia we had to go now because Lacey just called, and it didn't sound good. I rushed and got dressed and went back downstairs. Chase was dressed and waiting on the couch looking confused. He stood up and asked, "Leia, what's going on and who is at the Miller Point Motel?"

I told him, "One of Tee's ex-girlfriends told me she knew where Tee was and that someone was looking for her. She's meeting Tee at Miller Point Motel today; I was supposed to go with her but that was her on the phone telling me to come to the motel right away." We took the truck and headed for Duluth. It was a two-hour ride, so we took turns driving.

I drove for about thirty minutes and when I looked in the rearview mirror at Alicia looked like she had something on her mind. I asked her, "What's wrong?" She didn't say anything at first, but when she looked up at me, I could tell whatever it was it wasn't good. She had tears in her eyes and could barely look at me. I got off the freeway at the next exit and drove until I found a gas station and I pulled in and parked. I turned around in my seat and asked, "Alicia, what's wrong?" She said in a low voice, "Leia, let's step out of the truck for a moment. I have something to tell you."

We got out and I leaned my body against the truck, waiting to hear what she was going to say. I was worried because we never kept secrets from one another, so it must be bad. She took my hand I could feel her body trembling. She looked at me and said, "Leia, I wish to God I didn't have to tell you this, but I have to. Do you remember when you came home and told me and daddy about Tee being pregnant?" I looked at her and the tears were rolling down her face. I knew then that what she was about to tell was going to hurt. I slowly replied, "Yes."

"Daddy called me after he left." Then she paused and I couldn't help it the tears started forming in my eyes I tried to hold them back, but it didn't work. I was crying almost as hard as Alicia. She looked at the ground for a moment by then Chase had gotten out of the truck and was standing behind Alicia. She looked at me this time and my heart started to beat faster and faster it felt like it was going to explode "Leia, Jason was sleeping with Tee, and she is carrying his baby." I closed my eyes because they started to burn. Then I took a deep breath and asked her, "How long?"

Alicia looked at me like she was confused and the burning in my eyes had moved to my chest. I felt a million emotions all at once. Then I asked again, "How long have they been fucking, Alicia? I need to know how long." She looked at me paused and looked over at Chase then back at me. She asked me, "Leia, please just let it be. It was hard enough for me to hear it and then to tell you, so please just let it be." It felt like my chest was caving in I could hardly breathe but again I asked, "How long?" I was shaking. I was trying to stop, but it was out of my control.

She looked at Chase, then me. By now she knew I had to know. Then she told me, "Daddy said Tee was Jason's first." That was the final blow. I slid down the truck and sat on the ground and I could feel my heart breaking. I put my head in my knees crying, thinking everything we had was a lie. I didn't even know him. For years, he was sleeping with her and coming to lay in my bed and making me believe I was the only one. Then to have that bitch in my house, in my face and around our kids. I was crying so hard it was hard to breathe. I kept trying to catch my breath, but I couldn't.

Alicia knelt beside me and whispered in my ear, "Leia, you know Jason loved you. I don't know why he did what he did, but I know he loved you." I looked up at her and wiped the tears from my face and said, "Really, he loved me? How do you love someone and cheat on them the whole time you're together? Please help me understand that?" She looked at me as if she was trying to think of something to say but she couldn't come up with anything. Chase tapped her on her shoulder, and she stood up. He sat down next to me like he did when we were kids, and I was sad.

He put his arm around me and said, "Leia, I know there isn't anything we can say to make this better, so just know that we love you and we're here for you." I knew that, but it didn't make it any easier. I had just been hit with the worst possible news.

I looked at Alicia and then at Chase and said, "You know what's funny? I would always praise Jason for sticking by Tee when everyone else had abandoned her. Well, the joke was on me, huh?" I pounded my fist on the ground and yelled, "Fuck me for being so stupid" Chase grabbed my hand and held it tight. And said, "Leia, what he did isn't a reflection of you. Sometimes men do some strange shit and no matter how you play this out in your mind, you'll never be able to figure out why. But what you can do is look Tee in the face and ask her why." I sat there listening to every word he said, but that still didn't change how I was feeling. I felt humiliated.

Then the pain I felt turned into anger. I stood up so fast, it through Chase off. He slowly stood up. I went and got back in the truck, turned it on. Chase and Alicia looked at each other, then looked at me until I honked the horn and they got in. I drove at least another hour with the CD player blasting. I turned it up so loud that my body was vibrating. It had to be loud; I needed to be distracted.

I felt so many emotions when I saw the sign to the motel. I was ready to face Tee. She pretended to be my friend, even calling me her sister. How dare her play me! What kind of person does shit like that? Be my friend, but the whole time she's screwing my husband? When we pulled into the motel, it looked like a standoff. There were police cars everywhere and as soon as we pulled in the parking lot, the police that were outside looked directly at us.

Chase said, "Damn, what the hell went on here? It looks like the whole Duluth police department is here!" I looked at him and said, "I don't know, Chase, but they're all looking at us!" I got out the truck anyway; I had a purpose for being here and nothing was going to stop me from slapping Tee in her fucking face. Chase and Alicia got out and we walked up to where most of the police were.

Chase started talking to them. "I'm detective Chase Thompson of the St. Paul police department," Chase said while flashing them his badge. We're here looking for a friend of ours who's been missing for a few days, and we were told she was staying here." They looked at him then looked at each other. One of the officers replied, "Sure, I think I know who you're looking for."

He led us into the motel, and he stopped at the front desk in the lobby. Then he turned around and said, "You ladies can follow the gentleman to the other woman that's in the office and you can come with me." I wanted to say no, but Chase looked at me and I knew he wanted me to just do what the man said. We followed the other officer and once he opened the door, I saw Lacey. She jumped up and grabbed me and hugged me and began to cry. I really wasn't in the mood for this, but I hugged her for a second and sat her down.

I said to her, "Lacey what's going on?" She wiped her tears and started talking. You could tell she had been crying for a while, because she could barely talk. "I'm sorry but after I told you I would bring you here I got scared that if I did, Tee would fuck me up. After you left las night, I came up here. I didn't tell her I saw you; I just didn't want to be home when you came, so I stayed here last night. When we woke up, Tee wasn't feeling well so I went to get her some medicine and some food. When I got back, the door was opened I thought she was just getting some air. I put some food out for her and was about to put the medicine in the bathroom..." then she looked down and started crying.

I put my hand on her shoulder and she wiped her tears again and finished her story. "When I opened the door, I saw her in the bathtub on her knees with her hands tied behind her back. I ran over to help her, and when I pulled her up and she just rolled to the side. That's when I saw that she was shot in the head!"

I sat back, shocked by what she had just said. Tee was dead I couldn't believe it but, what really made me scared was the way I felt I wasn't sad. I was angry. Jason was dead so I couldn't get any answers from him and now the only other person that could at least face me was dead, too.

Lacey kept crying. I just sat there waiting for Chase to come back so I could find out what happened. It was taking Chase a long time to come down, so Alicia and I went outside. Plus, I was tired of hearing Lacey's crying. We sat on this bench in front of the motel not saying anything to each other. I just wanted to sit there and not hear anything.

A few minutes passed and the coroner came down with Tee's body. As he passed by us, I felt a wave of emotions, not for Tee, but for her unborn child. I couldn't be mad at the child. Right after that, Chase came out with the sheriff and stood and talked to him for a while, then waved to us to follow him. We went to the truck, and he got behind the wheel and started to drive.

Alicia and I both were waiting for him to say something, but he didn't. After about 20 minutes of silence, I got annoyed and asked, "Are you going to tell us what happened?" He didn't say anything right away, he just kept driving. He drove about another mile, then he got off the freeway and pulled into a parking lot. He looked at me and said, "Look, Leia, I know you think you can handle anything, but you're going to stop this Nancy Drew shit. And for the record, I think the person that killed Jason probably killed Tee. That Means he's very dangerous, not to mention determined to keep what he's done a secret. So, when we get back to your house, you're going to give me the answers I want."

I didn't say anything, because I had no intention of telling him what I found in those notebooks. And as far as being scared, I wasn't. I probably should have been, but I wasn't. The same way he wanted answers, well so did I. I would never know why Jason betrayed me, but I would find out who killed him and why. I have been to the edge of the cliff and back today, so I really wasn't in the mood for Chase's bullshit, and I planned to tell him just that once we got to my house. We drove the rest of the way not talking, but I wished we were because my mind was being flooded with visions of

Jason and Tee having sex or them sitting in my house laughing at my expense. I was so glad when we turned down my street.

As we were pulling into the driveway, Alicia said she had a date, but she was going to cancel. I told her not to. I know she wanted to be there for me, but I just wanted to be alone. Chase pulled into my driveway, and I got out. As I was walking to the door, Chase called my name. I turned around and by the look on my face he knew I wasn't up for any bullshit. I went in and took a long shower; I felt so dirty. Plus, I was trying to drown out the sounds of my sobs. Once the water turned cold, I got out. Alicia popped her head in to tell me she was leaving, so I got dressed and headed downstairs.

I grabbed two CDs and popped one in the CD player. As Luther played, I went in the family room, unlocked the liquor cabinet, and grabbed a bottle of Remy and a brandy sifter. I went back in the living room and sat on the couch and poured myself a drink. By the time the glass hit my lips, I was already in tears.

I was on my second drink when I heard the doorbell. I thought, "Shit, what now?" When I opened the door, Chase was standing there holding up a box of Twinkies. I smiled and he followed me into the family room. I sat on the couch and Chase sat next to me and looked at the bottle of Remy on the table. He smiled and said, "Damn, I guess Twinkies were the last thing on your mind!" I replied, "Today called for something a little stronger. Would you like a glass?" He looked at me then the bottle, then shook his head yes.

We sat there drinking a talking mostly about old times. Then I felt another wave of emotion and the tears turned on. He took my hand and pulled me to his chest, and he held me as I cried. After I had cried for a while, I put my head on his lap and feel asleep. When I woke up the next morning, I smelled bacon. I went to the kitchen and Chase; Alicia and Nate were hard at work. I looked at Alicia and waved her over.

I was surprised to see Alicia and Nate getting along, so I whispered in her ear, "You and Nate look like you're getting along." She whispered back, "Yeah, well after the way he gave it to me last night, I think we'll be getting back together soon!" Now that was a shock! Alicia and Nate hooking up? I said, "Wait, how did all this come about?"

She smiled and said, "We talked the day I saw him over here, then he started calling and the rest is what I said!" I was happy for them. At least someone's in love and I know for a fact that Nate would never do to her what Jason did to me. Then she hit my side and said, "When we got here last night, we saw you and Chase all cuddled up on the couch"

I knew where Alicia was going, but I wanted to stop her. The last time I slept with Chase was because I was hurt, and one of the reasons I really felt bad about it was that Chase deserved more. I wasn't about to go there again. If I was going to sleep with him again, I wanted it to be about love, not for revenge "We weren't cuddled up. I was crying and I fell asleep."

I walked away so that the conversation would end. I went and got a cup of coffee and walked up to my room. I shut the door, hoping that when I got back downstairs, they all would be gone. I sat the coffee on the nightstand and picked up the phone to call Nana. I really didn't want to call, but I really needed to hear her voice. Nana kept me sane in a world that was sometimes crazy. Cousin Dee answered the phone and said that Nana was in town with the kids. He tried to start a conversation, but I quickly said, "Thank you and goodbye!" I didn't want to talk to anyone but Nana. Then just when I was about to lay back on the bed, the phone rang. I started to answer, but I didn't. Alicia popped her head in my room and mouthed, "It's your mother." I wanted to tell Alicia to have her call me back, but I didn't if I wanted us to be closer. I had to keep the line of communication open. I picked up the phone and couldn't help but notice that she was very cheerful. I don't think I ever heard her so happy when she was speaking to me. She cheerfully said, "Hello, Sweetheart, how are you?"

I tried to fake a happy voice and replied, "I'm fine. I would ask you the same, but I can tell by your tone that you're doing great!" She replied,

"You're right, I am having a wonderful day. I thought I'd give you some time to yourself, but it's been a week and I was worried I hadn't talked to you."

I apologized for not calling her. I told her that I was just getting my thoughts together. I kind of wanted to tell her what I found out about Tee and Jason, but I didn't. I didn't know if I could trust her yet. My mother and I being close was new, so I had to make sure it was real. We talked a little while longer and I told her I was tired. I wasn't being dishonest; I really was tired. Before we got off the phone, she made me promise to have dinner with her the next night.

I sat there for a while staring at the walls in my room, thinking of all the times me and Jason made love in here, how I thought he was giving me all of him. When really, I was getting leftovers. Just as other thoughts started running through my mind, the tears started. I had cried so much my head was hurting. I laid back on the bed and I don't know why, but I snapped. I jumped up snatched the covers off the bed they flew all over the room. Then I went to Jason's drawers and started throwing all his things to the floor. Clothes were everywhere then I went to the bathroom and cleared the cabinets of all his things.

By the time I got back in the room, Nate, Alicia and Chase were all standing there. I just walked right by them and ran downstairs to his office.

I started with all his stupid ass books, throwing them off the shelf one by one. I was on my way to his desk when Nate stepped in front of me. He grabbed me and hugged me tight. I could feel my heart pounding. It felt like my chest was on fire and I had to finish what I started. I tried to pull away from Nate, but the more I tried the tighter he held me.

I finally gave up and yelled so loud the whole block probably heard me. "I want everything of his out of my house, Nate!" I don't want anything that reminds me of him here! Fuck this, I am selling this house! I hate him for what he did! How could he do that to me, Nate?"

I cried so hard my brain felt like it hurt. I was dizzy, and the next thing I knew I was waking up on Jason's couch in his office and they were all sitting around me. I didn't say anything, I just sat up. I looked around the room and it looked like a tornado went through there.

I got up and went to the hallway, got my shoes and left the house. I got in my car and drove until I saw the gate of the cemetery. Once I drove through the gate, I felt a burn in my stomach. I parked about a half a mile in and walked to Jason's grave. I stood there for a few moments and looked at his headstone. I promised myself on the way here I wouldn't cry. I stood there looking at his headstone. It read, "Beloved Son, Father and Husband."

I knelt in front of his grave and said what I came to say. "Jason, I don't want to hate you I really don't, but I don't understand all this. I know you loved me. I felt it in your touch, the way you looked at me touched my soul. So how could it all be a lie? Those feelings couldn't have been a lie. Why did you do this to us? I really want to understand. It sounds crazy, but it was easier to forgive you when you cheated with the tramp by your mom's house. Because I knew it was just a fuck, but with Tee I know it had to be more. You two were together almost every day. I used to be jealous because she knew a side of you that I would never know. Now she had you the same way I did, and that really hurts. Baby, tell me please! I need to know why."

I put my head in my knees then I felt a hand touch my shoulder. I was so frightened, but when I looked up it was Nate. He sat down next to me and said, "I don't understand why Jason did this, Leia, but most people live a lifetime and never know the love you two knew." I looked at him, then at Jason's headstone. I knew he was right, but I was still hurting.

We sat there for a while, and I headed home. As soon as we walked through the door the phone rang. It was Lilly, Tee's mother. I really didn't feel like talking to her so I told Nate to tell her I would call her later. I went upstairs so I could call Nana. Even though I really wanted her home, I knew she needed to be there for her sister. She had worry in her voice and she really wanted to talk about what Jason did. I told her I really was OK, but I was tired of thinking about it, so I really didn't want to talk.

Normally, I would have been mad at Nate for telling Nana, but not this time. I knew he was worried about me. Even though I knew she wanted to help me through this, I was happy she understood that I didn't want to talk about it now. We talked for a few more minutes and then I got in bed.

The first thing I did the next morning was call Lilly. She told me that she was going to cremate Tee because she had always said she didn't want to be buried. She asked me was I coming by today—she lived by my mother, so I told her I would stop by at 6:00 p.m.

I decided to clean up the mess I'd made yesterday, starting with my room. I was putting Jason's shirts and other garments in boxes when a piece of paper fell out one of the shirt pockets. I opened it; it had the four numbers 6125 on it. I put it in my pocket.

Once I had everything boxed up, I called AJ, a friend of Nana's who worked at a clothes closet. He said he'd be by tomorrow to pick up the boxes, so I went to the hallway closet to get all his jackets. I took them out and started to pack them away when I felt something in one of the pockets—it was a disposable camera.

I took it out and went straight to Walgreen's and put it in the One Hour counter. My first thought was it was pictures of Tee and Jason, so I went to the coffee shop across the street to wait to see what was on the camera. It was the longest hour of my life. I was almost running across the street when the hour was up. I paid for the pictures and went to my car.

I sat there going through the pictures. There were some of Allen Thompson coming and going, there were a few of James coming and going from the auto shop. There was one picture of Allen with a man, but the only one with his whole face was one of him walking away. The sun was too bright, so I couldn't see his face. I went back in and asked the photo guy if there was a way to fix it and make it clearer. He said yes, but they didn't have that kind of equipment.

I took the pictures and headed home. When I got home, Alicia was there. She asked, "How are you feeling?" I apologized about the other day; I felt bad that I had just lost it. Alicia said she understood and offered to make me dinner, but I told her I was going to my mom's house for dinner. I showed her the pictures and asked her was there anything she could do about the one that I couldn't see the man's face? Alicia replied, "I think I can get it a little clearer enough to make out the face." She took the picture and I got ready for my dinner date with Mother and left as soon as I got dressed, I had to stop by Lilly's, and I didn't want to be late meeting

Mother. When I pulled up, I saw a few cars in the front of her house. I sat there for a few minutes taking several deep breaths.

Finally, I got out the car and the woman that was sitting on the porch took my hand as I walked up. "Were you a friend of Tanisha, honey?" I was about to say no, but I caught myself and said, "Yes, I'm Jason's wife."

I went inside and Miss Lilly and her pastor was sitting next to her on the couch. There were a few others there, but I didn't know who they were. Tee was an only child and I never met anyone except her mother. Miss Lilly came and gave me a hug. She was crying and I felt so bad that I couldn't cry for Tee. I tried, but I just couldn't. Miss Lilly asked me, "Leia, why did someone kill my baby?" I looked at her and replied, "I wish I knew, Miss Lilly, I really do. I bet it was the same person who killed Jason,"

She hugged me again, still in tears. I wanted to get this over with; I didn't want to deal with what Tee did to me, not now. Miss Lilly went on and on, crying and praying, holding me the whole time. I was really hoping to get through this without mentioning the baby, but that was asking too much, because the next thing out of Miss Lilly's mouth was, "Leia, who was the father of her baby and why didn't she tell me?"

I took a deep breath and lied. "I don't know who the father was." I started to feel the same burn in my stomach that I felt when I found out

Jason was the father of her baby. I took a deep breath. I wanted to keep it together, but I felt like I was going to be ill. I just kept on talking, "She didn't tell me she was pregnant."

I left it at that and excused myself, but I didn't get away without being asked to speak at her memorial. I was so caught off guard. If I said no, she would ask why, so I said yes. On the way to my mother's, I kept saying to myself, "Why did you say yes?"

I got out and forced myself to smile all the way inside, so mother wouldn't notice that I was emotionally drained. Mother was in the same great good mood as the night before...if I hadn't known better, I'd swore she got herself some. She talked the whole way to the restaurant, going on and on about the community center she started volunteering at. She was giving free legal advice and mentoring teen moms.

I was proud of her, especially because she hated our neighborhood. She felt she worked hard to get where she was, and we deserved to live in a place that showed her position in life. Daddy wasn't hearing that, and we lived in the inner city. It was a nice area with big houses and mostly white people, but it was a few blocks from the hood. It was where his father had built his home, so that's where he was going to build his. It had changed since my grandfather built his house, but it wasn't a bad neighborhood.

Even though she hated living here, when Daddy died, she just couldn't bring herself to sell the house. She did cheat though—once I left, she bought a condo in downtown Minneapolis near her firm and stayed there during the week. We got to the restaurant it was packed, but mother had made reservations. Even if she hadn't, they would have found her a great table. She loved this place; it was another testimony to how much money she had.

As we were being seated, I noticed Allen Thompson and his wife, seated two tables from us. It was weird. As I was looking at him, he looked up and our eyes met, and he smiled and waved. I didn't want to wave back, but I did. We sat down, and before we could say a word to one another Allen was standing at our table. He smiled again, and said, "Hello, ladies!"

I know my hello was dry, but I wonder why my mother's was, too. He took my hand and said, "I'm sorry for your loss, Leia. If you need anything call me; you know that Jason was like a son to me." I wanted to snatch my hand away and tell him I knew he was full of shit, but before he could say another word, my mother said in a tone that I have never heard her use, "Thank you, but she has all the support she needs. Enjoy your evening."

He looked at her and she looked at him with disgust in her face. He just walked back to his table, and she looked like she was thinking but she started talking. "I know it's not right, but don't like that man...he's a snake!" The look on her face when she said that let me know she meant what she said, I wanted to ask her why, but I didn't. I knew there was a time and place for everything. This wasn't the time for that we were here to get closer. I would wait to find out what was behind that statement.

I wanted to lighten the mood, I asked her, "So, Mother, let me ask you something and don't get all defensive." She smiled and said, "Go ahead." I asked her, "Why haven't you ever dated?" She looked at me and I thought maybe that wasn't a good question. Then she said, "You know, Leia, I really don't know why. I just never thought about it. Your father was the only man that really made me feel special. Every other man in my life has either hurt me or disappointed me, so I guess I don't want to go from the love of my life to a loser."

I told her that I would be there to help her, and I'm not saying get married, but I want her to have someone to do things with. To my surprise, she was very receptive to the idea because she said, "Well maybe I will try dating; there is a new lawyer at the firm who is very attractive." I laughed and told her, "No, you don't date coworkers, but I do know that the principal at the twins' school is single!" I told her that when I got home, I was going to send him an email.

We had a great time at dinner. I dropped her off and made my way home. When I got there, I saw Chase's car parked out front. I was hoping he would've given me a few more days, but I knew he wanted the notebooks. I went inside and Chase and Alicia were sitting in the living room, looking like they were in the middle of a deep conversation. "Hello, you two, what's going on?"

Alicia gave me this look that let me know I wasn't going to be happy with what she was about to tell me. She stood up and walked toward me and whispered in my ear to come into the kitchen. I followed her, wondering what she had to say. Once we were in the kitchen she just blurted out, "Leia, don' be mad but I gave Chase the notebook." She stopped there like she was giving me time to digest what she had just said. I quickly replied, "Why in the world would you do that? You know why I didn't want him to see it."

She went on to say, "In return for me giving him the notebooks, he agreed to allow us to help. It's a good trade, Leia, you know it is. We need him and you know it, so stop being so damn pig headed." She was right, we did need Chase. It was only so much we could do. Alicia didn't wait for my reply; she walked upstairs. I slowly made my way back to the living room. Chase looked up as I came in. I guess he could tell what I was thinking by the look on my face. He got up and walked over to me and said, "Look,

Leia, I know why you were hesitant about giving me the notebooks. I saw

that Jason believes my father is the person who actually killed his dad."

Before I could say anything, Chase went on "Leia, I'm not going to air my

dirty laundry, but I will say this: me and my father are civil to one other. I

will investigate this as I would any other murder case." It surprised me to

hear him say that; I always thought Chase and his father were close. I

thought of what Nana would always say, "You never know what goes on

behind closed doors."

I asked Chase, "OK, fine. Where do we start?" He replied, "I want

you to go talk to Breanna. I paid her a visit, and she wasn't very

cooperative, but maybe she'll open up to you. I read her transcripts and

talked to the prosecuting attorney who handled her trial. He said he didn't

believe she did it, either. The prosecutor said they didn't find gun powder

residue on her hands or her clothes. Also, her fingerprints weren't on the

gun. All they really had was Charles's body at her house and her

confession."

Chase stayed for a while we went over what he wanted me to ask

Breanna. When he left, I went to Alicia's room and from the sound I

figured I'd better wait. I went in my room and took the picture of me and

Jason off the dresser and laid on the bed. I looked at it for a while,

remembering that day in the park. We were so happy. The kids were playing, and Jason and I were lying on the blanket talking. This guy walked over and told us he couldn't resist taking our picture, we looked so much in love he wanted to capture that moment for us. He was a photographer, and he took our name and address and a few weeks later we got this picture in the mail. I smiled as I touched Jason's face on the photograph. I thought about how much in love we were. That's why I couldn't wrap my head around Jason and Tee being together.

6 CHAPTER

I called Chase as soon as I woke up. He was pulling a few strings to get me in to see Breanna. Usually, you had to fill out a form and wait to have it approved, but Chase said he would have to call in a few favors to bypass the normal process. He said it was set up and I could go today and that the visiting hours were 11:00 a.m. to 7:00 p.m. I hung up and got ready. I stood in my closet wondering what to wear to visit someone in prison. I grabbed a pair of jeans and a T-shirt and hurried to get ready I wanted to be there at 11:00 a.m. I grabbed some snacks and some water and made my way to Shakopee Women's Prison.

I popped in a random CD for the 40-minute drive and the first song was Silk ("In My Bedroom"). I laughed because that was a song that Jason and I had made love to on a few occasions. The whole CD was slow and most of the songs were get-you-in-the-mood songs, so I took it out and turned on the radio. I made a mental note right there to buy a dildo. I never thought I'd need one, so the thought made me laugh.

The prison was this big brick building with bars on the windows and a wired fence around it. I walked into a waiting room with a lot of vending machines. There were signs everywhere. No, this, no that, don't do this and don't do that. I read every one of them. Chase told me not to bring anything but my driver's license, so I left all my jewelry and my wallet at home and put my driver's license in my pocket.

I had to wait in a line where there was only one guard to help 10 people. When it was my turn, I gave him my driver's license and told him I was there to see Breanna Morris. The officer said, "Oh yeah, we were told you were coming. So, you're writing a book about female killers?" I didn't know what he was talking about, but I figured that's how Chase got me in, so I played along. "Yes, I've always been interested in what makes a woman kill." He chuckled and said,
"Well, you're in the right place. Go through the doors and the guard will tell you what to do next."

I got a name tag and went through this big steel door. The guard on the other side of the door asked if I had any jewelry or any other valuables I told him no, then I was patted down given the rules and sent into another waiting area there was a lot of people, tables and more vending machines. Kids where playing and everyone seemed happy. I found a table in the back of the room that way I could see everything. There was a big desk with two guards seated there, one was on the phone, the other one was reading the paper, and another guard who was walking around.

I felt so sad for the women in here. I watched as a woman said goodbye to her kids; the smiles they once had were replaced with tears. I was so preoccupied by my surrounding I didn't even see Breanna coming over to my table. I turned and there she was standing at my table. I was so shocked because this was the woman in my memory with daddy. She was just older but still very beautiful; I see why she had the men around her sprung. She was taller than me, about 5'11" with reddish brown hair (almost redder than mine). She was light skinned almost white, and her eyes where the prettiest green I had ever seen. I stood up and held out my hand and said "Hello."

Breanna didn't shake my hand she said with a snappy voice, "You're not a writer."

I quickly said, "How do you know that?" She smirked and said, "Let's just say I know." Since she knew I wasn't a writer, I decide to cut to the chase. I told her, "OK, I'm not a writer. My name is Leia Richardson. I'm Jason's wife, his father was Charles." She looked at me and said, "Leia, I know who you are, but I'd like to know why you're here."

I could tell by her tone this wasn't going to go well, but I said, "I know you've heard Jason was killed and I believe by the same person who killed his father." She laughed but not a real laugh a fake nervous one. Then she said, "If you haven't noticed, I am serving time for killing Charles." I wanted to just give up but instead I said, "I know that, and I also know that you didn't kill Charles. What I can't figure out is why you confessed to a crime that you didn't commit."

She sat back and looked at me as if she was studying me. Then she sat up and popped a big smile and said, "Leia, look I'm paying my debit to society. I killed Charles—that's that!" I was getting frustrated, and this wasn't getting me anywhere. I said, "Look. I don't know what's making you stay here when you don't have to, but I will find out what I need to know. With or without your help."

She sat back again, but there wasn't any hesitation or smile when she said, "Do you think this is a game or some Nancy Drew novel? This is real life, and let's just say I am covering for someone. You're a smart woman… what could someone use to make a person admit to a murder they didn't commit?" I quickly replied, "I don't know Breanna, you tell me.

What does Allen have over you that would make you take the rap for Charles's murder?"

This time I sat back and studied her. Allen was my trump card, so I pulled it out. I knew from her tone she wasn't going to be any help, but I wanted to see what her body language had to say. She moved up to the end of her chair and leaned in close as she could get to me from across the table then said, "Look, Leia, I'm going to give you some advice and I pray that you take it."

She took my hands, and she had a look of concern on her face that I could tell was real. She went on, "Go home be a mother to your children, grieve the loss of your husband and move on. You're playing with fire, and I don't want you to get burned."

She stood up and walked away. She may not have told me what I wanted to know, but how she reacted when I bought up Allen told me that Jason was right—Allen was the killer. I needed to get more information on Allen, because the next time I visited her I want a few more facts.

I got home and called Chase. He said he had a few things to do before he left the office. We agreed that he would grab some takeout and come by around 8:00 p.m. That was good; it would give me some time.

I wanted to go see Joe, this old-school pimp who knew everybody. The word on the streets was that Joe brought Breanna up here to work the streets, but Charles took her from him. He lived a few blocks from James's auto shop, so I headed that way. This man was almost sixty but was still pimpin' hoes. When I pulled up, he was sitting on the porch with this girl. She had on a micro-mini and a halter top and her face painted up. She couldn't have been more than 16 years old. I walked up and he told her to go inside.

He smiled at me and said, "Um, girl you're fine-ass hell, lookin' good as yo' mama!" I ignored his stupidity, and plus everyone knows I don't look anything like my mother. I said, "Thank you, I guess." He stood up and came down the steps where I was standing and said, "So you lookin' for work?" I wanted to slap his tired ass, but I didn't. I just gave him this look that if he were smart, he would have seen the disgust.

I stepped back and said, "Look, I'm here to ask about Breanna." He walked back on the porch and sat back in his chair and smiled this devilish smile and asked, "Now why you want to know about her?" I looked at him and said, "I'm here to get information, not give it."

He chuckled and said, "Hmm, you want to know about Bree? Well, that's a bad bitch right there. I met her in Vegas; hell, she was only 16…at least I thought she was. She was clocking dollars, tricking with these white boys. Bree had this little pretend a pimp he had her lookin' like a two-bit hoe, as fine as she was. Shit, you know I had to scoop her up! I took her shopping, put her in some Chanel and shit like that. Once I did that, she was clocking real money. Shit, all of them rich dudes was all over her ass! Hell, I left Vegas with $20,000."

"I brought her to Minnesota, because we got some white men with deep pockets, plus she was beautiful. I knew I was going to make a lot of money, or should I say I thought I was going to make money. The bitch was here for a week and Charles swooped in and took her from me!" I was getting frustrated he wasn't telling me anything that I didn't already know. I said, "Look, that information is already in the streets...tell me something that's not."

He smiled and rubbed his hands together and said, "Well, baby girl, you know I'm about making money, so you want to know something, you gonna have to put something in my pocket." I looked in my wallet and I had three hundred dollars. I handed it to him, and he said, "Shit, girl have a seat," he patted the chair next to him.

"I'm gonna tell you everything I know about Bree. I'm sure you heard nice things about your father-in-law, but I'm gonna give you the real deal. Charles was a son-of-a bitch, and everyone knew you didn't fuck with him. Charles only cared about two things: his money and his bitches Sandra and Bree. Now with that said, let's talk about old Al. He's running around here talking like him and Charles was tight. Al was Charles's flunky, that's it.

He picked up money, dropped off product and that was his job. Bree was his top dope seller and Sandra was the stay-at-home type. Bree made money and a few babies, and Sandra raised them."

I interrupted him and said, "What? I thought Jordan and Jacob went to live with Sandra after Charles died." Joe went on, "Yeah, that's what they tell everybody who didn't know, but Sandra had those kids from day one. Now let me finish, cause I promise you, you'll get three hundred dollars' worth. Then we move on to James. Charles didn't show him no love either. Brother or not, he was a foot solder too, but see James wasn't the hustling type. Hell, two days after he started hustling, some niggas on the North Side robbed and shot his ass. You would've thought Charles would cut him some slack, being that he got shot and all. Nope. After James healed from his wound, Charles sent his ass back out on the streets, even though he knew that nigga was scared as hell. Then he beat his ass, cause Charles said James was a punk. Made that fool work for free for six months to make up for the money they took." Damn, I never knew that. James made it seem that him and Charles were close.

Joe kept talking and I let him. "Now then there's Samuel Peterson. He was a baller like Charles, but he feared Charles. He did his thang and tried to stay out of Charles's way. You see, there's a lot of unsolved homicides that have Charles written all over um. Now Beautiful, I have hoes to pimp, plus yo' $300 has run its course." Hell, I had more questions, but I could tell he wasn't going to answer them for free.

I asked, "Will you be around tomorrow?" He replied with a laugh, "Maybe, maybe not, but you better bring a lot of money cause I got some shit for your ears. Even some stuff about your dad." I stood up and looked at him and he still had his devilish grin. I wondered what he knew about daddy. He wasn't like Charles and his thugs—Daddy went to college and had his Doctorate. I dismissed what he said about Daddy, but I wanted to hear the rest he knew about Charles.

I got in my car shit it was 8:45 p.m. and I had two missed calls from Chase on my phone. I called him back and he said he was sitting outside my house with cold food. I told him I'd be there in five minutes. I got there and he looked a little pissed.

I apologized and told him I went to see Old Man Joe and he asked me, "Why did you go see him?" I looked at Chase and smiled and said, "Chase you know Old Man Joe is the fly on the wall. He knows all that goes on in the hood." Chase laughed and said, "Yeah, you're right! His ass is the fly on the wall! You'll have to tell me what the Polyester Pimp told you!" I laughed and replied, "I will!" We went inside I heated up the food and made us plates.

Chase was waiting to hear what I had found out from Breanna and Joe. I filled him in on my day. "Well, Breanna wasn't helpful at all, but when I brought up your dad's name, she just about jumped out her skin, so I know he's involved one way or another. Joe told me that Charles was an asshole and everyone on the streets including your dad and James were all scared of him. Did you know James got robbed and shot while dealing for Charles?"

He shook his head, I told him, "Well he did hustle, but he really wasn't good at it from what Joe said. Plus, he told me that once James recovered from his wounds that Charles kicked his butt and made him work for free for six months." Chase said "Damn, Charles was cold." I didn't want to say anything, but I added, "Yes, he was. Also, he had your dad spooked, too."

Chase laughed again, but even harder. Before I could go on, he said, "I can believe that my dad the dope man's flunky; running around acting like he ran the streets back in the day. I knew he was full of shit! I heard about how Charles used to punk his ass!"

I looked at Chase and said, "Can I ask you something?" He shook his head and asked, "Why don't you get along with your dad?" He looked at me and said, "Leia, it's a long story that I'd rather not share." I did mind, but I let it go. I could tell it wasn't something he wanted to talk about, plus I could understand back when mother and I weren't cool I didn't want to talk about it, either.

I told Chase that I was going to go back and talk to Joe. I told him he said he knew more plus he claimed to have info on my father. Chase didn't think that was a good idea. He said Joe probably didn't know anything else and that he was going to try to get me for more money. He was probably right, but I wanted to know what else he knew about Charles, plus what he knew about daddy. I left the Joe thing alone and we ate and talked over the game plan for the next day.

Even though she hated me right now, I needed to talk to Sandra. I told Chase I would go talk to her because I needed to get some more background on Charles and Breanna. Chase was going to see what he could find out about his father and James's relationship. We both agreed not to tell Alicia what Joe said about her dad.

Chase left and I called Nana. She sounded tired, so we didn't talk long. She said that one of my cousins was teaching Lil' Jay how to drive, and I thought, great now I'll have to hide my car keys. The twins were both asleep, so I told her I'd try again tomorrow.

I went upstairs and lit some candles and took a long bubble bath. When I got in bed, I fell fast asleep.

When I got up, the first thing I did was call the kids. They both sounded like they were having a ball, and we talked a while and then they said they had to go. The fair started today, and my other great aunt had a booth at the fair where the twins were going to be selling her honey.

I took my time getting dressed because I was nervous about seeing Sandra. Alicia's ass still wasn't home. I was happy for her and Nate, but shit, neither one of them have been helping. Alicia was supposed to talk to Sandra, but here we are four days later, and she still hadn't. I got dressed, cleaned up and did a few loads of laundry, but still no Alicia.

I really didn't want to see Sandra since she was very hurtful the last time, I saw her. It took everything holy in me not to curse her out and I was praying for the same today. I got in my car and put on a gospel CD to calm me down, so if she pushed, I would have the words of peace on my mind. I pulled up to her house and her husband was leaving for work. He stood at the gate waiting for me to get out the car, and when I got out, he gave me a big hug.

"I never really got a chance tell you how sorry I am about how Sandra acted at the funeral. Leia, she loves you and the kids, she's just grieving. Jason was her only child." I guess I never really looked at it like that; Jason was all she had, but that's still no excuse for her to treat me like that. "I know that, and that's why I am able to forgive her, but it still hurts."

139

He shook his head and got in his car. I walked slowly to the door. Before this I would've walked in, but today I rang the doorbell. She came to the door, and I thought she was going to close it in my face, but she didn't. She unlocked the screen and walked away. As I walked in, I could tell from the smell she was cooking. I walked in the kitchen a stood by the refrigerator. "How are you, Sandra? I know you don't want to see me, but I've been worried about you."

She didn't say anything at first; she just kept cutting her vegetables. I turned to walk out, because I didn't want to push, and it was obvious that she was still angry. "Leia, don't leave." She turned to face me, and tears were running down her face. "I'm sorry how I treated you, but he was my baby, Leia." I didn't say anything, I just walked over and gave her a big hug. We both cried. I knew she was hurting "I wanted to come to your house, but I was ashamed of how I acted. Please don't hate me, Leia."

"I don't hate you, Sandra, you're like a mother to me. Plus, you're the best grandma in the world!" She smiled and hugged me again. It was true—the twins love her so much and she's always been there for them. "They were very sad they weren't able to say goodbye to you."

"Where did they go?" she asked. "To Alabama to help Nana with her sister she had a stroke, they'll be back at the end of the summer."

"Now I really hate myself. My grandkids are going to be gone for the whole summer and I didn't get to see them before they left!" I gave her my aunt's number so she could call them. I knew that they would be happy to hear from her.

"Sandra, I'm not telling a lot of people this, so please don't tell anyone. I'm trying to find out who killed Jason. The police don't have any leads and they really don't have any way to find any either. You know how it is in the hood… what happens in the hood stays in the hood. I think I would have a better chance of getting information from people."

Sandra quickly said "Leia, I think you should leave it for the police. I don't want to lose you, too," I said. "I don't plan on going anywhere, so don't worry. Plus, Chase is working the case. I'm kind of like the side kick."

"Now that sounds a little better." She looked at me and smiled and I smiled back. I really missed her. She had been a mother figure for me for a long time, so I was happy to have her back. I needed to ask her about Charles and Allen and the rest of the players, but I had to be careful how I went about it. I knew that Breanna wouldn't be the place to start so I started with Allen. "I talked to old man Joe yesterday, and he told me that Allen and Charles weren't best friends like Allen tried to say. It was more like Allen was Charles's flunky."

"I haven't seen him in years how is Joe doing these days?" she asked. "He looked old, but can you believe he's still pimpin'? He had some young girl with him," I said. "He has always been a mess! We used to always say Joe was a runaway's worst nightmare," she said. "He was right about Allen. Look, I know he told you some crazy stuff about Charles and yes all of it is probably true. Charles was a very dangerous man out there in them streets. He didn't take any bullshit, but he sure did dish it out. At home he was different, so I just blocked out what he did out there in the streets.

"Plus, what could I do? Remember that story I told about how I found out about Breanna? I shook my head; it went different then I told you. I guess I was so used to sugar coating it for Jason that I did it to you," she admitted. "I was just putting Jason down for a nap when Charles came home, he had a baby in his arms. He handed it to me, and I looked at him for a minute and then I asked him who's baby this was. He looked at me and said it so nonchalantly, "Mines." I shoved the baby in his arms.

I walked in the bedroom and started packing. Charles came in the room and sat on the bed, and still calm he said, "You're my wife and I have taken care of you and given you everything you wanted and needed. Now I need you to do this for me. Remember the pastor said until death do us part!" Then he stood up and walked out the room. I sat on the bed for a

while I knew what he trying to say. That was the first time I feared Charles.
I didn't know who the mother was, and I didn't ask, then about a year later
James came over with Jordan when he was a month old. I asked him who
was their mother and he told me about Breanna. You know she never
came to see them boys. "Are you serious?" I said, she went on, "Yeah,
Jacob came straight from the hospital to me, and she kept Jordan for a
month then he came to me. It wasn't until she went to jail that I started
sending her pictures of them. They were her kids and she deserved to see
what they looked like. See, she never wanted them anyway—Charles just
wanted her to have them to prove to everyone that she was his. Now I
don't know this to be true, but rumor has it that she had another child that
she did want but had to give up because it wasn't Charles baby," she
explained. "Like I said, that's just what folks say, but me knowing Charles if
she did get pregnant by someone else, he would have killed her back then.

"Charles was very controlling to me and everyone around him.
Allen wasn't just Charles flunky, but an all-around punk. One day Charles
had come home for the night, and he had a rule when he's home that no
one from his outside life was to come here. I guess something had
happened with one of the dealers and Allen didn't know what to do. He
kept calling Charles, but he wouldn't answer, so he came over here. After I
opened the door, I grabbed the kids and took them in the kitchen because I
could see the look on Charles's face, so I knew he was angry. When I got

back in the living room Charles had slapped Allen across the face and told him to get the fuck out. Allen just walked out. I felt so bad for him I wanted to say something, but I had never seen Charles so angry that was the second time he scared me."

"How did Allen and Charles even hook up?" I asked. She told me that Charles and Allen grew up together back in Chicago. I was surprised because I thought they were from Minnesota. "No, they came here together see Charles's mother and father, who were both gangsters. The way I heard it, they were robbing a store and Charles's dad shot the owner and the police killed him. His mother was sent to prison for life, so Allen's mother took Charles in then she moved here. I don't know why, but I think Charles really didn't like Allen."

"Well, what about James?" I asked. "Where do I start? OK, Charles's mother's father was a preacher and he disowned her when she started getting in trouble with Charles's dad. When she went to jail, James was only two weeks old, so her father took him. He didn't want Charles— he was five and was already getting in trouble in school and had a smart mouth, so I guess he didn't want to take the chance on him. That's why Charles resented James. He had to be with Allen's family struggling while James had the good life Charles started hustling when he was thirteen."

"That's sad that he had a hard life, but why blame James?" I asked. "I don't know, but by the time James came up here, Charles was so far gone in the streets and the anger and bitterness had festered for so long that he didn't know how to react to James. The grandfather never let them communicate, so when James graduated from high school he applied at the University of Minnesota and got accepted. All just to be close to Charles. He wanted to know his big brother and he had this fantasy that they would reunite and live happily ever after...but Charles wasn't like James.

This was the third time that Charles scared me; I guess it's like they say the third one is the charm. Because this was when I knew that Charles's days on this earth were numbered. James had given Charles a key to his dorm room; you know he was his big brother, so he trusted him. I wish he wouldn't have done that, because Charles went there while James was in class and planted some weed in his room and called campus security. They kicked James's butt out of there so fast! That was the only time I did speak up I asked him why he did that, and he looked at me and said with no remorse or care, 'My granddad made sure my life was fucked up, so I'm going to make sure James's life is fucked up!' I was so angry! He had no right to do that! All James wanted to do was be a part of his life. I wanted to tell James what Charles had done but I was so scared if Charles found out he would hurt me."

"Did James every find out it was Charles who set him up?" I asked. "I don't know, but if he did, he never said anything. Charles told him it was probably some white dude. They didn't want blacks in college anyways and James believed him"

I sat there just amazed at what she had told me I really wanted to say it, but I didn't want to hurt her feelings…Charles wasn't controlling, he was a monster. How could you do that to your own brother? Wow, if Jason would have been like that, I would have taken my chances and left.

"Did Jason know any of this?" I asked. "No, I didn't want him to know that side of his father. He would hear stuff and ask me, but I would tell Jason that people were just trying to make Charles bigger than he was. I didn't want Jason to be anything like his father. I know this is going to sound crazy, but in a way, I was relieved when Charles was killed."

I didn't think it was crazy at all, because I would have been relieved, too. I could tell by her sadness that thinking about all this was draining her, so I changed the subject. We talked for a few hours, and I ate dinner with her. When I left Sandra's, I headed to Old Man Joe's. I wanted to know what he knew about my father, plus I want to hear more about Charles—the stuff Sandra didn't know about. When I pulled up, I saw a few girls sitting on the porch. When I walked up to them, they all started talking at the same time. I didn't know what they were talking about.

I interrupted them and said, "If you all talk at the same time I can't understand you," Then one of them stood up and told the rest of them to shut up. "Look, we ain't seen Joe since the day yo' ass was here, so what did you tell him cause his ass is gone!" I snapped back, "I didn't tell him anything! I was here to get information from him, which I paid him three hundred dollars for."

She put her hands on her hips and said, "Well, I don't know what happened then, cause when we came back last night all his stuff was gone and so was, he. Now what we supposed to do? We been sitting here all day trying to think of our next move." I thought, wow, they really must be dumb as Hell, if you worked for Joe, why can't you work for yourselves? But I didn't say that, because I really thought it was funny that they couldn't figure out what to do. I tried to keep from laughing and said, "Well, try the police"

She looked at me and snapped her head and said "Sure, we'll do that right now. Girl, is you crazy? What we gone tell them—we came home last night from working the streets and our pimp is missing? Shit, they'll have our ass in jail so fast! No thank you, I'm just gone find me another pimp."

I shook my head and replied, "Well, if you do see him let him know I'm looking for him." I got in my car and laughed so hard! Hoes without a pimp? What a tragedy! That thought entertained me the whole way home. When I got there, I wasn't surprised that Alicia wasn't home yet, so I went straight to the kitchen. There was a gallon of chocolate ice cream calling my name.

I plopped on the couch, grabbed the remote and started channel surfing. After about twenty minutes of T.V., I was depressed. It seemed like every show on was about love or people who were having sex…the last things I needed to be thinking about. You never realize how important sex is until you're not having it. I looked down at the ice cream container in my lap and it was half gone, so I closed it and ran to the kitchen and throw it away. The decision was made. I was buying a sex toy.

I went to the day room and got on the computer. I was too embarrassed to go buy one in the store, but this was different; no one would know but me and the online store. I went to this site "Play Time," and they had all kinds of stuff, but I went straight to the women's toys. I was surprised they had all kinds of them in any color you could think of. The site also had different sizes and shapes, some that vibrated, some that didn't. Hell, they even had ones you could put in water, and it still vibrated. I didn't know which one to choose. I was sitting there trying to pick a color; I figured that was an easy place to start.

I heard Alicia come in and call out my name. I yelled back that I was on the computer. I didn't care if she knew because she told me a few years ago she bought one so she wouldn't be surprised. But when she came in the day room, Chase was behind her. I jumped up and put my body in front of the computer to block their view.

"What are you trying to hide, Leia?" I gave her this it's personal look, but I don't think she got it. She was tried to move me from in front of the monitor and after a few tries she succeeded. She realized what site I was on, and she stood in front of the monitor. She smirked and said, "Um. I'm sorry, girl, you should have said something!" I sighed and replied, "I tried, but as usual, you don't listen!"

"I'll wait for you in the living room," Chase said as he walked away with a smile. I was so embarrassed! I hit her on the arm and said, "Thanks a lot. I really wanted Chase to know I was buying a toy!" She laughed, "Girl, please. He's grown and obviously so are you! I thought you told me you wouldn't ever buy one." I looked at her, "Girl, I never thought I would, but I'm so horny. I have a high sex drive. Shit, Jason and I did it four or five times a week, so I've been past due!"

I picked one with Alicia's help and went in the living room to talk to Chase. He wanted to know what Sandra had to say, but I told him I didn't want to talk about it while Alicia was here. He suggested we go to his house, but I told him it was getting late, and I had to be up early because Lilly called me, and she wanted me to stop by in the morning. I told him I would come by after that and he agreed. After he left, I went up to Alicia's room I wanted to know what her and Nate have been up to since neither one of them had been around to help.

I sat on her bed "So I haven't seen you around much," I said. She smiled and said, "I know and I'm sorry, girl. It's like we're meeting for the first time, and it feels good." I really understood what she was saying, it was like that every day for me when Jason was alive.

I smiled back and replied, "I know it feels good to feel loved. I'm so happy for you and Nate, I really am. I've been hoping for you two to be back together." She hugged me and said, "Thank you, but I have some good/bad news. I got a call from my friend Martin who has a big photo shoot in L.A but he can't do it, so he offered it to me. I'm sorry Leia, I said yes. I know that we're trying to find Jason's killer and when I get back, I'll help, but this is my big shot I have to take it."

I smiled and told her, "Girl, you better had said yes! Alicia, I wouldn't dare stand in the way of your dream; I know how long you've been waiting for a chance like this! Go, I've got it covered."

She said, "I was thinking about asking Nate to come with me. Would you be OK with both of us gone?" I replied, "Alicia you do know I'm grown, right?" She chuckled, "Yeah, but I know how hard things have been for you lately and I want to make sure you're going to be OK."

I reassured her, "Thank you for your concern, but I'll be fine. And, anyway, Chase is here." I went to my room so she could call Nate. I was happy for their new-found love, but it left me a little sad. I had that kind of love once, and I wasn't sure if I'd ever have it again.

7 CHAPTER

When I got up Alicia was already gone. I got dressed and headed to Lilly's, and when I pulled up, she was tending to her flower beds. "Good morning, Leia, come in!" She came to the sidewalk and gave me a hug. I followed her inside we went into the kitchen, and I watched as she poured me a cup of coffee. She gave me the coffee then she pulled an envelope from her apron and sat down.

She said, "The police brought some of Tanisha's belongings by yesterday. I found two letters in her suitcase, one was addressed to me, and the other was addressed to you." She handed me the envelope, and I took it and looked at it for a few minutes. I was so confused. I stood up thanked Lilly for the coffee and left before she could say a word. I wasn't trying to be rude to Lilly, but I really didn't want to think about Tee, nor did I want to read a letter from her. I had dealt with the fact that it happened Tee and

Jason had an affair and out of that affair came a baby, but I hadn't forgiven Tee.

I drove to Chase's house; it wasn't far from Lilly's. He lived in this three-story mansion off Grand Avenue. This guy had bought it and turned into three beautiful loft style condos and Chase had the one on the third floor. I pulled up and went upstairs. I swear I couldn't live here because you had to go up three flights of steep stairs. Chase was sitting at the table on his deck. He had made a full breakfast for us. I smiled. "All this for me?" He said proudly, "Yes, I thought since it was so early you wouldn't have time to make breakfast." As I sat down, I replied, "You're right, I didn't."

I looked at Chase then at all the food on the table I couldn't believe he did all this. Chase saw me looking around. "What's wrong?" I shook my head, "Nothing, I didn't know you knew how to cook." He said, "I learned from my mother. I spent a lot of time watching her cook." I joked, "I had almost forgotten that you were a momma's boy!" He laughed, "OK, I'll take that; but you know what they say about a man that treats his mother well." I laughed too, "Yes, I know what they say."

That saying was right. Chase was a bit of a momma's boy in school, and I think that's what made him so charming. Me and Alicia would always say he could charm the pants off a nun. I teased him awhile longer while we ate, then I told him what Sandra told me. We agreed at some point we needed to talk to James, but now wasn't a good time. We needed to gather up more information on all of them. I asked Chase if he could think of anything his dad may have told him about those days. He said he tried to talk to his father as little as possible. I could tell it was more than just family issues. Chase really hated Allen and I wanted to know why, but I didn't want to ask again.

I helped him clean the table and wash the dishes then I left. I wanted to go to the mall and get something to wear to Tee's memorial service. As I was on my way to the mall, I saw Lacy. She was talking to Lance, and they were all hugged up. I thought she was so in love with Tee and a lesbian to boot! I wanted to go over there and say hello, but I didn't, since the last time I saw Lance, we had words.

After about two hours, I found what I was looking for and I bought the outfit and headed home. On the way home all I could think about was Tee's letter I wondered what she had to say to me. When I got home, I put the letter in my kitchen drawer and went upstairs and got in the shower, hoping to wash away some of the pain I was feeling.

Halfway through my shower I heard something downstairs. I got out the shower put the towel around me and went to the door. I cracked the door open slowly and listened, I heard someone in Jason's office. I closed the door softly and locked it then called Chase. My heart was beating so fast! He wasn't in the office, so I called his cell—still no answer.

I dialed 911 and told the operator that someone was in my house. She asked if anyone else had keys to my house and I told her yes, but if it were any of them, they wouldn't be downstairs tearing up my husband's office. Before the operator could reply I heard someone coming up the stairs I told her to send someone fast the person is coming upstairs, then I hung up the phone got in the closet. I closed the door and hid behind the clothes that were hanging up. I heard the knob to my room being twisted I was so scared I just kneeled there in the dark praying, hoping that the police got there soon.

Then I could hear him pushing the door with his body. It got harder and louder, and I just knew the door was going to give way. Then suddenly it stopped. I sat there scared out of my mind, my whole body was shaking. Then I heard pounding on the door again but this time it was the police. I jumped up and ran to the door I opened it and there were two officers standing in my doorway. I yelled, "Did you catch him?"

They shook their heads and said "No, when we got here your back door was forced open and your front door was wide open so he must have gotten scared and ran. We'll go through the house and the neighborhood, but he's probably long gone. By any chance did you get a look at him?"

With tears running down my face, I replied, "No. I was in the shower, and I heard noises downstairs." As I was talking Chase was running up the stairs. He said in a panic, "Are you all, right? I heard the call on my scanner!" Through my tears I managed to say, "I'm OK, but someone was at my door trying to get in!" Chase took me and hugged me I think he was shaking more than me.

One of the officers said, "We'll look around and see if he left behind any fingerprints or anything. Detective Thompson can you take her downstairs and see if anything is missing." I didn't want to leave his arms. I think he knew that so he told them to check around and take the evidence and he would do the walk through later. They agreed and went downstairs I stood there in his arms sobbing. After I got it together, I said, "We've lived here for years and never had any problems. Hell, all our neighbors are white."

This is my home, a place where I always felt secure and now that security was gone. Someone had taken away my husband and now my sense of security. That was the last thing that this person would take from me! I swore to myself right then that Allen would pay for what he had taken from me.

We went downstairs so that we could see the damage. Jason's office was the only room that had been touched and I went in and looked around. It was worse than when I had my breakdown in there. Chairs were knocked over; glass was broken from the pictures and the couch was cut on the bottom. Books were thrown everywhere. I took a deep breath and looked at Chase and started picking up the mess. We didn't say anything to one another as we cleaned. It took two hours to clean the office and once we were done, I went outside and sat on the deck. I needed some air and to think I knew one thing for sure—whoever broke in was looking for something and I knew what that something was. Chase finally said something "Leia, you know they were looking for those notebooks." I took a deep breath and said, "I know, so Tee must have told him where it was."

I looked up and saw Sandra was walking up, and from the look on her face I could tell she knew what happened. Her husband was a paramedic, so he must have heard the call. She came and hugged me she started talking a mile a minute. "It was this investigating stuff that led to this wasn't it, Leia? Please leave this to the police." I didn't say anything because I knew I wasn't going to stop looking into it, so I just let her talk. Chase asked Sandra to stay with me until he came back because he wanted to go by Tee's and see if her house was hit as well. Plus, I think he didn't want Sandra to get on his case.

After she talked for what seemed like hours, she started to make dinner. I went in the living room because I needed to sit in a quiet place; I had more thinking to do. When I sat on the couch, I noticed a file on the table it had "Tanisha Jackson" written on it. This must be the file Chase got from the Duluth police. I opened it and there were statements from other motel guests. The couple in the room next to Tee's room said they heard arguing an hour or so before they heard the police. They said they heard two female voices and a male voice then after about 15 minutes they only heard two voices, a woman and a man. That meant that Lacey was in the room when Tee was killed, and she had to be a part of it because why would he leave her alive?

Lacy lied and I planned to confront her, I went through the rest of the file, but there wasn't anything else that was helpful. Sandra finished dinner and I ate it even though I wasn't hungry. As we were doing the dishes, Chase came in he said Tee's place had been hit to that confirmed someone was looking for the notebooks. We talked about Lacey and how she was more involved than we thought, plus when I told Chase about seeing Lacy with Lance, he decided that we should go to Lance's house.

We took Sandra with us because he didn't want her there by herself. On the way he said I should be the one to go to the door. I told him that wasn't a good idea being that I hated my half-brother, and I knew the feeling was mutual. When we got to his house Lance wasn't home, so we sat outside and waited for him. We saw Lance pull up, but Chase told me to wait until he went inside before I went to the door because he didn't want Lance to see him. I went up to the door and rang the doorbell. Lance came to the door and stood there looking me up and down I swear he made the hair on the back of my neck stand up. He smirked and said, "Princess Leia, what can I do for you?" I asked, "May I come in?" he looked at me and laughed then his face turned serious. "No, you may not. Remember, I'm not welcome in your house, so you're not welcome in mine." Then he shut the door in my face. I wanted to knock and when he opened the door to slap the shit out of him, but I didn't. I went back to the car and told Chase, "I told you so!" Chase decided he would talk to Lance tomorrow, and we went back to the house. I knew once Sandra knew about the break in, she was going to stay, and she did, even though Chase told her he was staying with me. She wasn't trying to hear that she went in Alicia's room and laid down. I let Chase sleep in Lil Jay's room, which was next to my room. I changed and got in the bed today was a long day, but I knew tomorrow would be worse... it was Tee's memorial service.

8 CHAPTER

I woke up feeling very uneasy. I hadn't written anything I was I going to say at the memorial and to be honest, I really didn't want to say anything at all. I was almost done getting ready when Chase knocked on my door and offered to go with me. I said yes so fast that Chase had to laugh. I was happy he asked; I really didn't want to go alone. I finished getting dressed and went downstairs where Sandra was sitting on the couch reading the paper. She looked up at me and I knew she had something to say. "Leia, come here and sit with me for a minute." I was hoping that she wasn't going to start in about Tee. She didn't like her and her being dead didn't change that.

"Leia, James told me about Jason and Tee." I took a deep breath and looked down. I was trying to hold the tears back, but as usual they came anyway. Sandra lifted my head and looked me in my eyes. "Baby, you don't owe her anything. You don't have to go to her memorial." I said softly, "I know Sandra, but I need to do this. I need to put this behind me and maybe going to her memorial will help to forgive her."

I knew she didn't understand it, but I didn't care. I had to go. I've always been a very compassionate person, but for some reason I couldn't feel any compassion for Tee, and that scared me. I didn't want to hate her or have any negative thoughts toward her, not for her sake but for my own.

When we got to the church everyone was already inside. When Chase and I walked in, I saw Lilly she was standing in front of Tee's picture. When I saw the picture, I felt sadness, but I still couldn't shed one tear for her, and I tried very hard to. Lilly came over and gave me a hug and I whispered to her that I wasn't going to speak, that I was just here for support. I wasn't angry at her anymore. The anger had passed, but I wasn't about to go up there and say good things about her—she betrayed me.

Chase and I sat through the whole service then we gave Lilly our condolences and declined her offer to come to her house before leaving. I wasn't surprised that Lacy didn't show up to the service. Chase wanted to stop by his house to grab some of his things and informed me that he'd be staying at my house until Alicia and Nate got back.

We went inside Chase was surprised because there was a message on his answering machine from his father. He said his father never called him. I wanted to ask him to call him back while I was there, but I didn't. I could tell by his reaction just getting a message from his father disturbed him. I looked around while he packed. His condo was decorated very nicely. I asked, "Who's your decorator?" He laughed and asked, "Why do you ask that? Couldn't I have decorated?" I joked, "Unless you have a little sugar in your tank, I think this has a woman's touch!" He laughed again and said, "Well, we both know how much I love the female anatomy, but to answer your question, my mom decorated for me." I joked again, "Yet again another example of momma's boy syndrome!"

We both got a laugh out of that one. He finished getting his things while I waited, I pick up his photo album and looked through it. There were a lot of pictures of us when we were kids and pictures of Chase with his mom, but none of Allen. I really wondered what happened between Chase and his dad. It seemed when we were young, they were close. My dad coached the basketball team at our school and Allen was at every game and when the team had a banquet, Allen and Mary where always there. Chase came in and took the photo album off my lap.

"Do you remember this?" He went to the back of the photo album and handed it back to me. It was a picture of the princess ball at our church. Pastor Williams threw it every year for the girls in our church. We were in the third grade and Chase was my escort. We looked so cute! Him in a little tuxedo and me in a gown. I told him I wanted a copy of the picture; I had forgotten about that. My mother had a picture of the ball on her mantel. My mother wanted Chase and I to be together, but it didn't work out that way. I must admit before I met Jason, I wanted that too.

Chase and I went back to my house to drop off his things. He had some work to do, so he dropped me off at my mother's. I hadn't seen her since our dinner, so I wanted to hang out with her. I rang the doorbell but didn't get an answer, so I used my key to let myself in. She wasn't home, so I decided to go check out my old room. It was just as I had left it the night, she kicked me out. I sat in the chair by my bed and looked around. Being here brought back so many happy memories and some sad ones. Like how daddy would sit in this very chair and read to me every night or how me and Alicia and some of the girls from school would have sleepovers in here.

But the memory that is so strong and very painful was the night I was told if I didn't have an abortion then I needed to leave. I remember sitting here waiting for James and Jason to come get me, trying to process what had just happened. I tried to talk to her, but she went in her room and shut the door she wouldn't talk to me at all. I had to shed a few tears because that was a day I tried to forget. I thought it was the day I lost my mother forever. I'm glad that didn't hold true, but it was a long road to where we are now.

I went over to my dresser all my old clothes were still in there. I went through everything, then I got so excited I couldn't wait until Jada got home. I was going to bring her in here and let her take anything she wanted. Then I went to my nightstand where I kept all my important stuff in the drawer. I knelt next to the bed and felt under it and got my key I kept it hidden between the box spring and the frame. I opened the drawer all my things where still there this is where I kept all my keepsakes. There where letters from Jason and things I collected from my outings with daddy and Nana, concert ticket stubs and my scrapbook. I opened my scrapbook and on the first page was a picture of Jason, Chase, Rodney and Perry. Under the picture it said, "PBC Boys."

I laughed because I had forgotten about that. One of the staff members at the rec center used to call them that it stood for the Pretty Boy Crew. They were the finest boys in the neighborhood, and they would hang out in front of the rec. I took this one so I could show Chase.

I took out all the postcards from the places daddy had taken me and put them to the side so I could show the kids. I picked up the letters from Jason and set them aside also. I wanted to take them. There were some pictures of me and Alicia and Chase from school, and I took those, too. I had a pile of things from my room I wanted to take so, I went to the pantry to get a bag to put them in. Mother always used to keep handle bags in the bottom drawer in here and I looked, and she still did. As I grabbed one, I heard someone coming toward the pantry. I thought it was my mother, but when I turned around, I discovered it was Lance. I got this uneasy feeling and my heart started pounding.

I asked him, "Where's mom?" He replied, "I don't know. She wasn't here when I got here." I walked toward him so that I could get out of the pantry, because it felt like the walls were closing in on me, but he didn't move so I could pass him. He just stood there. I said angrily, "Excuse me!" He just stood there with this weird smile on his face. This time I raised my voice and said, "Are you deaf? Move!" I was hoping that would be enough, but it wasn't because he didn't move.

By this point I was angry. I tried again, "Look, I'm really not in the mood for your shit today, so get the fuck out of my way!" He laughed and said, "I know the world revolves around you and everything, but I don't." Then he started walking forward so I was backing up until my back was against the wall. I was so scared, but I didn't let him know it. He touched the end of my hair, and I slapped his hands away. Then he touched my hair again and said, "I always wondered where you got this hair. It's all silky and red." I slapped his hand away and snapped at him, "That should concern you because?" He replied, "I'm just saying you got white girl hair and if you were two shades lighter, I'd swear you were a mixed breed."

I snapped at him again, "Is there a point to all this because I really would like to get out of here. Move out of my way!" I tried to push him, but he grabbed my arms and pinned them to the wall, and he leaned and whispered in my ear, "Tell me your fantasy and I'll tell you mine." I started shaking because I knew where this was going. I hated Lance and he always made me feel uneasy, but I never ever would have thought this is what was on his mind. I screamed, "Let me go now!" But he didn't. He licked my neck, and at that point, fear took over. I lifted my knee and hit him in the nuts so hard he let me go, and I ran out of the pantry.

By the grace of God, Mother came in the door right then. I hugged her so tight that I think she felt me shaking. She quickly asked, "Baby, what's wrong?" She took my face in her hands and looked me in the eyes, then looked at Lance as he walked out of the kitchen smiling. She knew something wasn't right, but I didn't expect her to do what she did next.

She yelled, "What did you do to my daughter, Lance?" He smirked, "Nothing." Then he sat on the couch and grabbed a magazine and started flipping through it. Mother walked over to him and snatched it out of his hands and said, "I know fear. I lived it at the hands of my parents, then at the hands of your father, and I swore that neither me nor my children would ever know that kind of fear. How dare you bring it into my home!"

Lance jumped up before she could finish and yelled, "You swore that your children wouldn't live in fear? You're a fuckin' joke! When you left, who the fuck do you think dad used as a punching bag? So, save that I'm-a-good-mom for your whore daughter!" Then he walked out. I always thought it was just talk, but Nana would always say the "devil don't hide; he looks you square in the face" She was right.

Mother dropped to her knees and started crying. I knelt next to her and held her and then she looked up at me and asked, "Did he hurt you?" I knew then that she knew what had happened or what almost happened. I shook my head, "No, but he tried to. I'm sorry, Mother. I know you want a good relationship with Lance."

She looked at me and said, "Leia, don't be sorry. He was wrong, not you, and I can't have him trying to hurt you. I never thought that his father would hurt him. I left him because if I would have taken Lance, his father would've killed me," she explained. "It doesn't make sense. His dad treated him like a little king—he wouldn't even allow me to even yell at Lance. He never raised his voice at him! I don't know, Leia. I really have a hard time believing that he beat him."

I wanted to say something to comfort her, but I didn't know what to say so I said nothing. I just took her hand and we sat there quietly. I knew there was something off about Lance, but I never thought that he was sick. Chase came and I didn't want to tell him at first, but I did once we got back to my house. He sat there for a minute like he was trying to process what I had just told him than he said, "That dude is sick." He made a call on his cell and told me to keep the door locked and left. Ten minutes later, Sandra and her husband were at the door.

Sandra came and gave me a hug and said, "Leia, are you all, right? Chase called and told me to come over here right away." I told her what happened with Lance, and she was angry. She said she hoped Chase went to go kick his ass. I sat there wondering where Chase had gone, and I started to worry. Chase had a temper when we were in school—he was always getting into fights with the white boys. They would try to jump him, but he would kick all their asses no matter how many there were.

After about an hour, I was worried. I called his partner and told him what happened and where Lance lived, then I told him I'd meet him there. Sandra wouldn't let me go alone, so she sent Albert with me. When I pulled up, I could see two people fighting. I stopped in the middle of the street and Albert, and I jumped out of the car. I was trying to grab Chase and Albert was grabbing Lance, but we couldn't get them apart.

Frank got there a few minutes after we did, and he grabbed Lance around the neck, so Albert and I grabbed Chase. As Frank was holding Lance, Chase walked over to Lance and said, "If you ever so much as look at her wrong, I'll kill your sick ass!" Frank told Chase to leave, and I told Chase I'd meet him at the house.

The whole way home, Albert was talking about how he wished he would have been able to get a few punches in, but all I kept thinking about was my mother. Lance is her son and she tried to act as if she were OK, but I know how I would feel as a mother to have your son try to do something like this to your daughter. As much as I hated Lance, I was sad that all this happened. Mother needed him in her life; his father had kept him from her for all these years, and now she's lost him again.

Chase was already there when we pulled up. Damn, he must have been flying to get here so fast. I got out and walked over to him; he was leaning on the car touching his lip. I told him to come in the house so I could put some ice on it. We went inside and I made him an ice pack. He took it and went upstairs. I wanted to follow him, but I could tell he wasn't in the mood for talking.

Sandra and Albert left, and I went upstairs I knocked on the door, but Chase didn't answer. I went to my room and took a shower. It felt so good. When I was done, I heard a knock on my door. I put on my robe and opened the door and Chase said, "I'm sorry, but I needed so time to cool down. Leia, I want you to know I'll never let anyone hurt you. I don't care who it is." I gave him a hug because I knew he meant every word.

He went back to his room, and I got dressed and sat on the bed for a minute. Then I got up and went to his door and knocked. When he opened it, I said, "I don't want to be alone tonight." He took my hand and pulled me in the room. We laid down and he put his arms around me, and we fell asleep.

I awoke to noise upstairs. I jumped up because I knew that Alicia was home. She was putting her things away, and when she saw me, she ran over and gave me a hug. She asked, "Are you OK? What the hell is wrong with Lance?" I told her, "Yeah, I'm fine. How did you know?" She replied, "The phone was ringing when I came in and Sandra told me everything. That sick fucker needs to be in jail!" I said, "I'm trying to let it go for my mother's sake. I know this has to be hard for her." She replied, "I heard Chase kicked his ass. He should have put a bullet in him."

I wanted to change the subject, so I asked about the photo shoot. I'm glad I did—she went on and on about how much fun it was and how amazing the pictures turned out. She did so good they booked her again, so she was going to be leaving again in a day or two. I was happy for her, but she was a little sad because she felt like she was needed here. I let her know there was no way I would ever let this, or anything come between her dream. She had worked too hard for too long not to make her dreams a reality.

If It Don't Kill You…

I had a whole pile on mail with my name on it. I went to the kitchen, got a cup of coffee and set the pile of mail in front of me. As I was about to open the first piece, Chase came in and got a cup of orange juice. I began opening the mail, and hoped he would say something… I was feeling a little weird about last night.

The first 10 or 12 pieces were just junk mail, and then I came to a big white envelope from my college. I opened it and looked at the leather-bound case. I rubbed my hand over the gold writing that said my school's name. I had forgotten that I called and told them I wouldn't be attending the graduation due to my husband's death. My mentor was very disappointed. I waited so long for this, but at this point I wasn't in the mood to celebrate. I opened it and I was proud when I saw the words "Master of Behavioral Sciences." This is what I've worked so hard for. I took a few moments to take it in then I moved on to the rest of the mail.

There were a few bills, so I went to get the checkbook, when I came to a big yellow envelope addressed to Jason. It was from the licensing department. Inside were some papers and on the top was a post it that read, "It was good to hear from you. Here's the information you asked for. P. S., if you ever get divorced, call me, lol. Melody." I took it off and laughed out loud. It was the license for James's Shop. Why did Jason want a copy of James's business license? I looked at it and nothing jumped out at me, so I whispered to Chase while I handed him the papers. I didn't want Alicia to hear. "What do you think Jason was looking for?" He looked at the papers one by one then I saw his eye pop open a little wider when he got to the fourth page. Excitedly I asked, "What?"

He stood up and said, "We need somewhere where we can talk." He pointed outside. I got up and followed him outside and we headed for the garden. I sat on the bench that faced the house so we could see if Alicia came out. Chase quickly said, "I know what Jason was looking for." He showed me the page he was looking at and it said, "second party license" and in the name line it listed Allen Thompson. I sat there for a minute. I couldn't believe it...Allen was James's business partners. I always thought James was the only owner. I said, "I'm confused. Why would James and Allen be business partners?" Chase replied, "I don't know, but I plan to find out. I'm going to talk to James myself." I said, "I think that would be a good idea, Chase."

Chase went inside, but I sat there looking at the steppingstones leading to the garden. There were words engraved on them: love, faith, peace and family. I kept thinking, what in the hell is going on? First, I found out Jason was sleeping with Tee and now this.

I got up and went in the house and told Chase to get me in to see Breanna today. She may not want to tell me why she's protecting Charles's killer, but I had some questions that only she could answer. I got dressed and waited for Chase to give me the go ahead to see Breanna. He came in and told me I could see her, so I headed for Shakopee.

While I waited for Breanna to come to the visiting room, I told myself I wasn't going to allow her to blow me off like she did last time. She came to the table with this why-are-you-here-again look on her face. "Leia, why are you here? I told you last time to raise your kids, use that Degree of yours to play with other people's lives, and leave mine alone." I wanted to ask her how she knew I had a degree but I didn't.

I quickly replied, "I plan to do that once I find the person that killed my husband. Look, Breanna. I know you have a reason for not saying who really killed Charles, but you hiding this secret led to the murder of my husband." She looked down and then looked at me and said, "Don't you think I know that; not only do I have Charles's death on my head, now I have Jason's When he came to see me, I told him some things that would lead him in the right direction, and look what happened to him," she said. "Leia, I will not put your life on the line. I'm here doing life and that is my reality, but your reality is different. You don't have to be in danger… you have a wonderful life! Live it and let this go. I know you loved Jason but getting yourself killed won't bring him back! Please stop this now, because they'll kill you, too."

She got up and walked away, but I couldn't let her. I needed to

know why Allen and James where partners, because if Allen did kill Charles

what did James have to do with it? I went after her and grabbed her arm.

She stopped and looked at me, then the guard came over and told us to sit

down so we did. I pleaded with her, "Breanna, I need you to answer just

two questions for me, please?" She looked so frustrated, but she agreed.

I asked, "I found out that Allen and James are partners in his repair

shop. Why would James be partners with Allen?" She didn't look surprised,

she just sighed and said, "Allen and James where both foot soldiers. So

maybe once they stopped stomping the street together, they decided to

open a shop. Now what's your next question? I'm missing my show." Then

I said, "I want to know how you knew my father." She looked at me for a

few moments and then she started to stand. She quickly said, "I didn't know

your father." I told her, "Please sit back down, or I'll stand up and make a

scene." She looked surprised, because the face I made she knew that I was

serious.

Then I continued, "Listen, I know you knew my father. I

remember you being in the park with us, so I know you knew him." She

leaned forward and looked me in my face. "Leia, I'm not going to answer

your question because I know you're not going to like the answer. Stop

digging through the past, because you're going to bring out a whole bunch of mess." She walked away and this time I didn't stop her. She was right; I didn't think I was going to like her answer. Whatever the reason she was around daddy, it wasn't good.

On my way home, I went to Sister Ann's house. She was Nana's best friend, and nosy as hell, so I knew she would have some answers. When I got there, she was just about to walk her dog, so I joined her. I tried to ease into it by hitting her soft spot: Buttercup is her baby, so I started there. "Buttercup has gotten so fat, Sister Ann! What are you feeding her?" She laughed and said, "Child everything I eat! You know this my baby! Now, what's on your mind, because you look troubled." I swear her and Nana were mind readers!

I took a deep breath and said, "Sister Ann, I know you hear a lot, so I was wondering if you heard anything about Charles, Jason's father." She looked at me and gave me that smile she usually gave when she was about to tell you the business. "Come, child. Let's sit over there on that bench, because I heard a whole lot about him and them fools, he had running behind him." We sat down and she tied Buttercup and got comfortable. She looked behind her as if someone was watching her and whispered, "Now don't tell your Nana I was being messy. You know she don't like gossip!"

I assured her I wouldn't say a word. Then she said, "Well, I heard that Charles was a mess and treated them boys that worked for him bad— even killed a few of 'em. But they were the lucky ones, cause the fools that didn't get killed got it worse. Like Allen, Child. Charles treated him like he was a little boy; cussing him out all the time and I heard he even slept with his wife!" I said, "What! Charles slept with Mary?" That was hard to believe. Chase's mom is like, super saved. Ann continued, "Oh yes, honey, sweet as honey Mary. See, even saved folk fall Sometimes, you have to understand why she did it. It's really kind of sad. Mary was always in the church, and when she met Allen, she didn't know what he was doing out in the streets. He treated her good—wined and dined her and then he popped the question. Because he was so sweet Mary said yes.

The sweetness went away after they were married, because that's when Charles really started treating Allen like dirt. When Charles started treating Allen bad, he would take it out on Mary. After many years of that, she got tired. Plus, Chase was getting older, and she didn't want him to keep seeing Allen beat her. I heard she made a deal with Charles; she would sleep with him if he got Allen to stop beating her. It worked, cause after that, the beatings stopped." I really felt bad for Mary, because she must have been desperate to do something like that.

I asked Ann, "Do you know if Allen knew about it?" She replied, "Child, that I don't know, but there were a lot of folks in beds they had no business being in." Ann had this look on her face like the tea she was about to spill was too sweet, so I had to ask her "Who else was creeping?"

What she told me threw me completely off. "Well, I heard that Sandra and James had a thing going on behind Charles's back. They say she was trying to get back at Charles for being with that yellow girl." I don't know if I believe that, plus Nana always said Sister Ann had a thing for stretching the truth. I got up and said, "Wow, I knew James and Sandra were close, but I would have never guessed they were sleeping together." Ann gave me this weird look and said, "Child, there is a lot of secrets hidden around here... you just have to know where to look to find them."

I walked her back home and headed home. On the way I kept thinking about what Sister Ann had said, I had to find a way to bring it to Chase. I knew he wasn't going to want to hear it, but I had to tell him. I was already keeping things from Alicia, and I didn't want to do that with Chase.

When I got home, Chase was still at the house. He said Alicia was gone and that she was at Nate's. I was glad. I told Chase what Sister Ann had told me and he just sat there for a moment. I didn't say anything—I waited to see what he was going to say. After a minute he said, "I could really use a drink." I went and got him a shot glass and the bottle of Remy. I knew he was going to need more than one shot.

He poured a shot and took it to the head and said, "Thanks, you asked me why I hated my father; now you know why. I watched him beat my mother for no reason. One day when I was five, we were sitting on the couch and mom was reading me verses from the Bible. My father came home, walked right up to her and **slapped her across the face. He hit** her so hard she flew back. Then she just stood up and said, 'Come on baby, let's go night-night.' When she put me in bed and gave me a kiss, I asked her why daddy hit her. You know all she said was, "Your daddy's a good man, but the devil just has a hold of him right now." When she left my room, I could hear him beating her even more and I've hated him ever since.

"One day when I was about 11 or 12, my dad came home and asked, 'Where's your mom?' When I said church, he said, 'Yeah, that whore should pray, and hope God forgives her ass!' So maybe she did, and knowing Charles, he probably threw it in my dad's face. That bastard forced her to have do something like that."

I put my arms around him. I knew how he felt, because now I knew for sure that Breanna knew my father and he probably had an affair with her. I thought the moon and sun set on my father's head and I hated thinking that he might have done something like that to my mother. We sat there me holding him for hours than we went upstairs. I needed him the other night and now I had to return the favor.

9 CHAPTER

I got up and slid out of bed and headed to my room. I threw on a sweatsuit and went to Sandra's to ask her about what Miss Ann had said. Sandra's a lot of things, but she's never been a liar, so I knew she would either not talk about it or she'd tell me the truth. I was glad that Albert had already left for work. Sandra was in the kitchen reading the paper.

She looked up and with a big smile she said, "Hey baby, how are you?" I smiled and replied, "I'm fine, how's your morning going?" She said, "Girl, I'm here, praise God!" I sat down and thought about how to go about the task ahead. I said, "Sandra, I need to ask you something. I really hate to, but it's important." Sandra smiled again and replied, "Leia, you know you can ask me anything."

I just wanted to say it and get it over with "I was talking to Sister Ann…" As soon as I said that Sandra's rolled her eyes, because she knew

Miss Ann was the gossip queen. I went on, "I hate to repeat this, but she said that you and James had an affair."

Sandra shook her head and said, "Well let me tell you this now: she is dead wrong. See James would come over when Charles was with Breanna. He needed a friend; someone who he could talk to. Besides, Charles had him running with them thugs, he needed someone he could trust," she said. "So yes, he was here a lot when Charles wasn't, and no Charles had no idea, because if he did, he would have broken James's neck. People saw him coming and going so they thought we had a thing, and after about a year or so, James started to think so to. One day out the blue when I was standing by the sink he came over and tried to kiss me. I slapped the hell out of him and girl do you know he had the nerve to try to snap? He said I was nothing but a fool staying faithful to Charles while he was over there fucking Breanna. I told him that was Charles's sin, and he would have to answer to God, not me. Then I showed him the door and didn't speak to him again until Charles's funeral."

I laughed and said, "Wow, James had a crush on you!" She laughed and replied, "You know after that happened, I realized that!" She also told me that Mary slept with Charles so that he would stop Allen from beating her. I wonder if that's true?" Sandra said, "You know James told me about that while we were friends. I never asked Charles, because at that point,

Leia, I really didn't care what he did...I was just glad he didn't want it from me. Because, and excuse my honesty—but sex with Charles was rough, if you know what I mean. Knowing Charles, he probably did sleep with Mary. The funny thing about that is she didn't have to sleep with Charles to get him to stop Allen; Charles hated for a man to put his hands on a woman. One day we were driving down the street when he saw this man beating this woman. Charles stopped the car and jumped out. Girl, he beat that man so bad once we left, I wondered if he was dead!"

I said, "I wonder if he told Allen he slept with Mary?" Sandra thought for a moment then replied, "You know he probably did. Charles was a hit-them-below-the-belt kind of man. "Then I asked her, "Did you know that James and Allen were business partners?" She looked at me as if I had slapped her, then she replied, "Honestly, I didn't think they were close. James made it seem like he couldn't stand Allen! James said Allen was always telling Charles shit that he had done so he could score brownie points."

We sat there for a while talking about Allen and James. She told me to go talk to this guy named Tony who used to run with them, and he would be able to tell me more about Allen and James. He owned a pool hall downtown, so that's where I headed. I checked my purse and I realized I had forgotten my cell at home. I knew Chase was probably wondering where I was, but I wanted to go talk to Tony.

When I got to the pool hall, I was glad it was daytime, because this didn't look like a place I'd want to be at night. There were only a few people in there and it looked like they were up to no good. I looked around and saw there wasn't anyone over 30 in there, so I asked the man at the bar if Tony was available. He said T wouldn't be here until after five. I wiped the pay phone down with a towelette that I had in my purse, because it looked dirty.

I called Chase. He was at the station and said he would meet me at the pool hall after his meeting, so I went to Nate's mom's house to wait. When I got there, she was on her way out the door she told me to lock up when I left. I hadn't been over here in years. I grabbed her photo albums and I looked through all the pictures. There were so many pictures of me and Nate when we were kids, and lots of pictures of mom and dad and Nana. She even had lots of pictures of her when she was pregnant. Right then it dawned on me that I never saw any pictures of my mother pregnant. Then I remembered that she was doing her internship at her firm's New York office while she was pregnant. Daddy said he would fly down once a month to rub her stomach.

I was getting bored, so I started rambling. She had all kinds of cool stuff from the 70s, like pictures and knickknacks. Nate would always say he felt like he was living in the 70s and now I see why. As I was about to go crazy, Nate came in. I filled him in on everything I had found out, plus I told him about the break in. Then he filled me in on what he had found out. "That coincides with what I found out, Leia. I think James is foul! Him and Allen are thick as thieves and if Allen killed Charles and Jason, I doubt that James didn't know."

I was hoping James and Allen became close, because Charles treated them both like shit. I was praying that was the case. I replied, "Nate, I don't think James would kill his own brother and nephew." Nate said, "Look, Leia, you said it yourself that Charles treated him like shit. Plus, he ruined his college career. Leia, niggas have died for less! You knew Jason— do you think Jason was going to just drop it because his uncle was also involved? No, Jason wanted answers and I think he confronted James. Who else would have been able to get close enough to Jason to shoot him in the head? Leia, I've rolled with Jason too many times. He didn't trust no one when he was out here in these streets, so he wasn't going to let nobody get in his ride. Even the sloppiest nigga knows you don't let nobody get in your ride! That makes it easier for someone to rob your ass, so it was someone he trusted!"

I hated to admit it, but Nate was right. Jason was big on loyalty, so I know he wasn't going to drop it, especially once he found out James was involved. The only thing was that I knew James and I can't believe that he would do something like that, especially to Jason. He loved him like a son. I told Nate, "Look, I know what you're saying, Nate, but I can't believe James would kill Jason. I just can't. Nate, I need more evidence to lead me to believe that James was involved. If James is involved, what is Alicia going to do? I swear, Nate, why does it seem like the closer we get to the truth more lives that are being destroyed?"

Nate replied, "Leia, finding the truth always comes with a price." He was so right, and the price was getting higher. How in the world am I supposed to look at James as if he were a suspect instead of family? Chase came and Nate and I filled him in, and he agreed with Nate. If Allen and James were best buds like we thought, then it's more likely than not that James was involved. I told Chase I was going to see Breanna again now we had information. Plus, I needed to keep at her because she was bound to break.

Chase left me at Nate's mom's house, and they went to go to see James. He told me things were going to get tight. He had to smoke them out, so he was going to treat James like a suspect. To shake a branch and see who falls out. I didn't like the idea of Chase treating James like a suspect because I wasn't totally convinced that James was involved.

I waited patiently for them to come back, but I felt so uneasy about this! But if this would produce a viable lead then it was worth it. To occupy my time, I grabbed another photo album and this one had pictures of May in her heyday. There were a lot of pictures of her at different parties. As I was going through the album, Aunt May came home. She was excited to show me all the fun she had back in the day. She said that Charles and his crew would through these big parties at this club called the Zone where all the players hung out. As she flipped the page, I saw a picture that caught my attention; it was a picture of James, Allen and Charles. James and Allen were standing behind Charles and the looks on their faces were very troubling. They both had a look like they despised something. May said this was the weekend before Charles was killed.

I asked her if I could take the picture and she said yes. Chase called and told me to meet them at my house. He said James wasn't at the shop or at his house. He asked me to wait outside in my car if he wasn't there because he had to make a stop first. I headed home. On the way home I kept looking at that picture, wondering if James could really do something like that. Charles may have been an ass, but he was his brother. Plus, James had other options.

Chase and Nate hadn't made it to the house yet, so I waited in my car with the doors locked. I saw lights behind me, so I turned off the car and got out. I thought it was Chase, but it wasn't it was James. Even though I knew what I knew, I couldn't treat him any other way than as an uncle. All we had were some suspicions that I was hoping wouldn't be true.

As he walked up, he said, "Hey Leia, why are you sitting out here?" He seemed his normal self. I replied, "Well, I don't know if you heard, but someone broke in a few days ago. I was here alone, and it scared me really bad." He said, "I heard. I'm sorry I didn't stop by sooner, but I was so busy."

Now that wasn't like him. He normally would drop everything for family, plus the whole time he was talking to me he didn't look me in the face. That made me sad, because I knew from my communication classes that when someone close to you is lying to you they won't make eye contact. I shook the feeling I was having because this was James, and I was hoping he wasn't involved.

I asked him, "Can we go inside? it's really hot out here." As we went inside, he asked me, "So, did they take anything?" I replied, "No, I don't think they found what they were looking for." Chase was shaking branches, so I was going to shake some, too.

He asked, "You know what they were looking for?" This was my chance, so I said, "I think so. I found out after the funeral that Jason was looking into his father's death, and he kept notebooks with the things he found out." After I said that, I searched James's eyes. I wanted him to look me in my face, but he was all over the place. I could tell in his voice that I shook the right branch. He rubbed his forehead and asked, "Um, do you have the notebooks? I would love to see them because far as I know, Breanna killed Charles." I quickly said, "No, I don't. I gave them to Chase, and they're evidence now."

He said, "Well, I think it's a bunch of bull. Jason knew who killed his father and she's in prison for it." I want to shake a little more, so I threw him a curve ball. I replied, "Yes, Breanna is in prison for it, but that doesn't mean she did it. I've been visiting her to try to get her to tell me who she's covering for, and I think I might be close. We'll have all the answers, because I think whoever killed Charles killed Jason to keep their secret." He was trying to act indifferent, but it wasn't working. He was jumpy, especially when Chase and Nate walked in.

James got up so fast he almost fell. He said, "I wish I could stay, but I have a meeting." He kissed me on the cheek and tried to leave, but Chase stopped him. "I have some questions for you. Can we step into the kitchen?" James quickly said, "I really have to go. I have an important meeting to get to." Chase replied, "You can answer them here or at the station; it's your choice."

James looked at Chase like he was going to hit him, but he didn't. He just walked into the kitchen while Nate and I stayed in the living room. They were in the kitchen for an hour. I don't know what Chase was asking James, but I could tell James didn't like it because we could hear James yelling. After that, James came storming out the kitchen and left slamming the door behind him.

Chase came out of the kitchen with a troubled look on his face and shaking his head. He said, "Leia, I know you love James and think he wouldn't do something like this, but when I questioned him, he acted like a guilty man. I've been doing this long enough to know James is involved. I don't know how involved, but he is caught up in this somehow." I sighed and replied, "At first I thought he wasn't, but after talking to him myself I know you're right."

Chase thought it was too dangerous to stay at the house, so I hurried and packed a bag we went to a hotel. I was expecting motel chain, but we went to the W, which was a five-star hotel. He reserved a suite and he said he wanted us to be comfortable. I will admit I was the suite was huge. It had two living rooms and a dining room, a full bath and a half bath, and a king-sized bed that was so soft that I thought I was going to melt. The only thing was there was only one bed. He said that was the only suite they had for the week, so he would sleep on the couch.

I put my things away and showered. After I got dressed, I went into the living room and Chase was sitting on the terrace looking at the sky. I went out and stood next to him and without him saying a word, I knew exactly what he was thinking. No matter what was going on, Jason's murder and all we had found out wasn't far from my mind. Tonight, I just wanted to act like all was the same and the people we loved were still the same people they were before all this, so I grabbed Chase's hand and took him inside. I called China Palace and ordered us some take out and turned on the cable and found a funny movie. We needed to laugh and pretend that things were all right.

10 CHAPTER

When I woke up, Chase was gone and had left a note saying he had

some work to do. It also said I should stay in the suite, and he would call

later. I called and ordered myself some muffins and coffee. I sat on the

terrace and thought about Jason. I know it must have broken his heart to

know that James may have had something to do with his father's murder.

Then I had to think about the fact that if James did have something to do

with Charles's murder, then it's more likely than not that he had something

to do with Jason's death. How in the world could he do that to his own

family? What's crazy is that Charles was the one that everyone considered

the monster. I was starting to feel sick… just the thought of James doing

this made me ill.

I got up and went inside to put some water on my face. As I was

about to go into the bathroom, there was a knock on the door. It was a

masseuse—Chase had arranged for me to get a massage. The masseuse set up and I changed and laid on the table, and for the next hour my mind was cleared, and I was totally relaxed. When he was done, I tipped him and said a thank you to Chase. I really needed that. I was so relaxed I wanted it to continue, so I took a long bubble bath in the sauna tub.

When I got out the message light on my cell was blinking. I checked my messages and there were two messages; one from Nana and one from Alicia, she sounded very upset. I called her back and as soon as I heard her voice, I knew James had talked to her. She was almost yelling, "Leia, what the hell is going on? My father called me all upset saying that Chase basically accused him of having something to do with Charles's and Jason's deaths! Why would you let Chase do that? Do you really think my father would do something like that? For God sakes, that was his brother and nephew! My father isn't some fuckin' monster!"

I tried to calm the situation and I said, "Alicia, no one is saying he is, but you have to understand that we got some information that proves that Allen and James were tight back then and they still are." I went on to tell her everything that we had learned about Allen and her father. She just sat there listening and when I was finished, there was a long pause.

She quickly said, "You know what? I don't care what you say. I know my father and I thought you did, too. He would never do something like that, and I swear to you I will never forgive you for this. I stood by your side while everyone was talking about how you were a whore for getting pregnant. I stood by you when you cheated on my cousin with Chase. I even held my tongue when I heard that your dad had cheated on your mom and that you were the product of that affair. So, before you go trying to put everyone out on Front Street, you need to get your shit together!"

Then she hung up, but at that moment I wasn't thinking about Allen, James or even Jason. I was thinking about me. I sat there for a while in a daze. I was trying to figure out if she just said that to hurt me or was there really something to this. My mind was going a mile a minute. I thought about my hair it was super long and curly my mother's is thick and long so that fit. My skin tone is a light caramel brown, and both my parents are dark brown so there wasn't any reason to doubt. I'm 5'7" my father was 6 feet, but my mother and every other woman on my father side was short. I was going around and around, pacing back and forth around the suite, trying to figure this out. As I was standing on the terrace still pacing and talking out loud, Chase grabbed me by my shoulders.

He yelled, "I've been calling for the past four hours! Why haven't you answered the phone?" I looked at him and then I thought, OK he can confirm this. He's known me my whole life. I told him what happened with Alicia, then I got to the part about me. I knew Chase and by the look on his face he already knew what rumor I was talking about. I was almost in tears when I asked him, "So you heard that, too?"

He sat me down and said, "Leia, why are you tripping about this? Alicia just said that to get to you because she was hurt. You know what folks around here do! They're always spreading rumors!" I asked, "But why would they say that, Chase? That my father had an affair and that I was conceived from that affair?" Chase replied, "Leia, let it go. It was a stupid rumor." I couldn't because I knew him, and I knew that he wasn't telling me everything. Chase would do anything to protect me; even lie.

I quickly said, "I will if you answer one question for me, and I swear Chase don't lie to me. Who did you hear this from?" He paused and started to walk away, saying, "Leia, let this go, please. "I stood in front of him with tears in my eyes and asked him again. "Who did you hear this from?" He looked down, then at me and said the one name I didn't want to hear. "Sister Ann told my mom about it." I felt a lump in my stomach and this time instead of just feeling sick, I threw up. I think I already knew the answer, but I asked it anyways. "Who did she say was my mother?" He looked at me then sat down with his head down for a minute. "Leia, don't do this... some things are better left unsaid."

I stood in front of him "This is my life and I deserve to know. I want to know! Who did she say was my mother?" He took a deep breath and looked up at me and broke my heart. "Breanna." I stood there trying to hold it in, but I couldn't. I went back to the bathroom and threw up some more. I washed my face and brushed my teeth and got dressed. I told Chase I wanted him to take me to my mother's house.

Chase said, "Leia, why just leave this alone? Just because Sister Anne said it doesn't make it true. Wasn't she wrong about James and Sandra? Don't do this to yourself or your mother. You two just got back together." I heard him, but I didn't care about all that; I had to know the truth. This was my life and my truth, and I had to know.

I yelled, "Chase, I'm going to ask her. She has always been straight with me, like it or not so if it's a lie she'll tell me that. But I need to hear it from her." I headed for the door, and I didn't give Chase the chance to try and stop me again. He followed me, and on the way there he tried to talk but I turned on the radio and turned it up. When we got to my mother's house, Chase said he'd wait in the car. I was praying the whole way in the house that she was going to tell me that this was all a lie.

When I went inside, she was in her office. I knocked on the door and walked in and soon as I entered, her face lit up. That made me feel good. I walked over to her and gave her a big hug. I swear I didn't want to let her go and even though we went through some things, I loved my mother so much. "Leia, baby, what's wrong? Your heart's beating so fast! I hope you're not still worried about the Lance thing?" She pulled me away from her and looked at me. I replied, "No, it's not anything like that. I have to ask you something I really don't want to ask, but Alicia is upset with me, and she said something." She stopped me, "Leia, you know people say things out of anger, so I wouldn't give it any weight." I wanted to leave it at that, but this would eat me up—not knowing would drive me crazy, so I had to ask her. I told her what Alicia had said, then what Chase said Sister Anne had told his mother. She took my hand and sat me on the couch. She put her head down and then looked up, cleared her throat, and begin to talk. "I'd prayed that I would never have to tell you this, but I promised myself if this day did come that I would tell you the truth.

She sighed and went on, "I know your father told you about Lance's father and how he hurt me, but he didn't tell you everything" I could see that this was hurting her and even though this has forever changed me this didn't change us. She was still my mother, and I didn't want her to have to relive this. I stopped her and said, "Mother, don't I don't care." She stopped me, "You need to know…you have a right to know the truth. So, back to that night. I was tired of it; I couldn't take one more day of being with him. When he came home, I had our bags packed and I was leaving, me and Lance. I knew he would beat me, but this time I was calling the police. He laughed and then started beating me. It lasted for a few hours, but when he was done as I walked away to clean myself up, I said, 'I'm still leaving.'

He called his mother and took me and my bags and Lance and put us in the car he dropped Lance at his mother's house. Then he started driving for hours and then he stopped." She was twisting her hands the whole time she was talking, but then she stopped, and tears rolled from her eyes. I took her hand and told her she didn't have to go on, but she started talking again.

"He dragged me out of the car, and he beat me again and then he ripped off my pants and stuck a screwdriver inside me and twisted it. Then he spit on me and said, "Now go, bitch, but you're not taking my son and you'll never give anyone a child, you whore!" Then he just got in his car and drove away. I thought I was going to die out there. It was dark and there wasn't anything for miles. I prayed to God that if he let me live, I would do something with my life. I guess I blacked out and when I woke up, I was in the hospital and guess who was standing next to my bed? He whispered in my ear, 'If you tell them, it was me, I swear I'll kill you.' I didn't tell, either.

I waited until the night before I was going to be released, then I left. I knew Miss Anderson had moved to Minnesota, so I called her, and she said I could come. I never thought I would meet someone like your father and fall in love, but I did, and he loved me. He knew everything and he still loved me. Even though I had trouble showing love and even had trouble accepting it sometimes, he still loved me. I had gotten so caught up in law school and trying to forget what I had been through, that I neglected your father. After years of therapy, now I know I was trying to push him away because I didn't feel like I was worthy of being loved. But your father didn't go; he just kept loving me and telling me I was going to be OK. I really can't tell you when the affair started or how long it lasted because I didn't ask him. I accepted the fact that I was so caught up in making something of myself that I had pushed my husband into the arms of another woman. He promised he would never do it again and I promised to make more time for him.

Things were great. We were spending more time with each other, and we both were happy. Then a few months before I was to start my internship in New York, your father came home I was in our room writing a paper. He sat on the bed and told me that the woman he had the affair with was three months pregnant. He said she was leaving town and would give us the baby when it was born. Leia, I didn't even think about it: I said yes. I want you to know why I said yes. Lance's father had taken my ability to have another child. I knew your father wanted a child and he knew I would never be able to give him one and he still married me. Now I had the chance to have a child and it didn't matter how you came to me. All that mattered was that you were ours. I went to New York, and he told everyone that I was pregnant. The only person besides us that knew the truth was Nana.

I had arranged for Breanna to come to New York, and she stayed with me. She had you and the only thing she asked for was $10,000, which she needed so that Charles won't be so mad. Leia, I know you have heard some really bad things about her, but she really is a nice person that's been through some really bad things. She could have taken the money and never came back to Minnesota, but she did because of her boys. I love you and I know all this is hard for you, but we all loved you, and Baby, I will always love you You're my daughter. I hope this won't change the relationship we're trying to build."

I gave her a big hug and reassured her, "Mother, I love, and I know you love me and I want to continue to build our relationship. Breanna may be my biological mother, but you'll always be my mom." We hugged and I told her I had to go; Chase was waiting outside. I also told her something that I had just decided while she was talking. I was going to Alabama for a while. I needed to get away from here I was trying to find justice, but it seemed all I've done is ruined people's lives.

I got in the car and cried. I didn't want to cry in front of my mother because I knew she was already in pain, and if I cried it would have made her feel worse. I think from the tears and the fact that he sat in the car for an hour that Chase knew the rumor was true.

We got back to the hotel, and I went to my room. I laid there thinking how in the world could Breanna be my mother. Chase came in and sat on the bed and said, "Leia, I know this has got to be hard for you to deal with, but I want you to know I'm here for you." I told him, "I know Chase, but I need my grandmother. I'm going to Alabama for a while I have to get out of this city." He replied, "Leia, running isn't going to change anything; it just prolongs the pain." I told him, "I'm not running. I just need some time to take all this in. I'm going to deal with it, but I can't do it here." Chase replied, "I understand that, and I think you leaving for a while is a good idea. You'll be safe while I put a case together."

He laid down behind me and put his arms around me. I needed to be held because I was so hurt. I got up the next morning and was able to get a flight out at noon. I didn't even call Nana and tell her I was coming. I told Chase to call her after he dropped me off at the airport. I didn't want to tell her over the phone everything that was going on. I needed her to help me make sense of everything.

I packed and Chase took me to the airport. I stood there saying goodbye and I didn't want to leave. I felt so guilty about how I was feeling about Chase. I gave him a kiss on the lips that I think shocked him. I didn't give him a chance to say anything; I just turned and walked to the line. Chase was another reason I was going away. I felt like the more time I spent with him the more I was feeling for him. I didn't know if the reason I was having these feelings was because I was vulnerable, or if the feelings that were always there had just gotten stronger, but I didn't want Chase to get hurt. I got on the plane and put on headphones and listened to music the whole way there. I didn't know if Nana would be at the airport when I got there, so I had planned to call her once I landed.

Chapter 11

I got off the plane and went to baggage claim and found my luggage. I turned around to go find a seat so I could call Nana. As I was sitting down, I heard her voice. I looked around and I saw Nana and my cousin Leroy standing by a row of seats. I ran over there and gave her a big hug and I had a mental break down right there in the airport. I told her everything starting with the whole Tee and Jason affair then to the last blow—the fact that I had found out Breanna was my birth mother. I was talking so fast; I really didn't know if she was able to understand everything until I was finished.

Nana looked at me and softly said, "Leia, take a deep breath. She turned and spoke. Leroy go and get her water or something." She sat me down and she said, "Leia, I'm not even going to tell you how foolish it was for you to be trying to be some amateur detective. You know it wasn't the best thing for you to be doing. You know that old saying, 'What's done in the dark always finds its way to the light?' Folks say that for a reason. I hate secrets, because some secrets can ruin people's lives, I never wanted to keep the truth from you, but it wasn't my decision to make. That was up to your father and mother."

"Leia, your mother has been through a lot it. It started with her parents and ended with that demon she was with. She never knew real love until your father, but she loved you both so much. When she brought you home, I had never seen her so happy she would sit and watch you sleep when she came home. She couldn't show you how much she loved you, but she did, so don't judge her. She did the best she knew how to. Far as your father, he was wrong for cheating on your mother and he was disappointed in himself, but everyone makes mistakes. His mistake brought more joy than pain. Now the whole Tee and Jason thing, I'm just at a loss about that one. You're going to have to give me a minute to process that."

"I'll move on to Lance. Leia he was raised by someone who has been possessed because you must be to do the things, he did to your mother so now we see the apple didn't fall far from the tree. That's no excuse for what he did, but it just explains it. Now the James and Allen thing I just pray that James didn't do what it sounds like he did. Leia, I know Alicia is upset with you but if James did do this, then he needs to stand up and take responsibility for it. His actions have helped destroy many lives, so he should pay for that. This world is a mess and it's going to get a lot worse, so all you can do is pray, live a good life, follow the Lord and hope none of this craziness touches you."

I knew she was right, but it still bothered me. We got into Leroy's truck and made the long drive to the farm. When we turned into Sunny Tree Farm, there were trucks and cars parked along the road and I could see smoke and a whole lot of people. It was a family tradition that when someone came into town the whole family had to come and food was a must. I was cool with that—I needed lots of comfort food and what's better than a southern cookout?

When we pulled up Jada and Lil' Jay came running and almost knocked me down. We hugged for a while, and I swear I didn't want to let them go. I kept kissing them and Lil' Jay didn't even say anything—usually he would be trying to tell me he was too old for that—but not today. He just kissed me back.

I made my way to the back of the house most of the family was there. The one thing that made me proud and very happy was that our family was very close. My whole family came to Jason's funeral even though they didn't agree with his lifestyle. We stuck together, good or bad. We were a family and if you needed help or even if you didn't, they would be there in a flash.

I couldn't wait to go see Auntie. She was always so full of life and to see her in a wheelchair broke my heart. She was sitting on the back porch looking at the pond and I walked over to her and gave her a hug and a kiss. She looked up at me and smiled. I was surprised how clear her speech was. "Here's my angel! Girl, you know that you remind me of the sun; you have a glow to you that makes folks feel good even during bad times." She would always say that every time I came down and told everyone I was her pick and that was that. I loved her, too. She was the spitting image of Nana and they both had this way of making you feel special and oh so loved.

I didn't want to cry but the tears came. She took my hand and said, "The world can be crucial, and the devil is always working against us, but there is power in prayer so pray and then keep on praying so that God is always close to your heart. When things get so bad that you feel like you can't go on, God will carry you."

"Look at me—the doctors saying I should be dead or in some coma—they call it a mystery. It ain't no mystery! It's God's grace that I'm here and able to talk and have all my thoughts. Don't give the devil no more power. Give all the mess that's going on to God and he'll deal with it for you."

I laid my head on her lap I was glad I came. I could breathe down here; the air felt fresh not all thick like it did back home. I went out and

205

joined everyone and laughed and had a good time. I was really trying to forget all the things that happened.

It worked for the whole day but when night came it was a different story. Everything came flooding back. I tossed and turned for hours then I just gave up on sleeping. I went out back and sat down by the pond and looked at all the fireflies and cried. Cousin Leroy came and sat down and put his arm around me. "You're like me, Cousin. When I can't sleep, I like coming out here to watch the fireflies. They just look like they're having so much fun! Then I look at the water and watch the light from the fireflies bounce off it. Then before you know it, whatever the problem that was keeping me from sleeping has just passed. Look, I know you were going through some things back at home and I know it's hard to see the silver lining. But if you let all of it weigh you down, you'll never get up."

Then he kissed me on my forehead and went inside and I sat there watching the fireflies as they danced around the sky. Then I looked at the water and the lights looked so beautiful. I sat there for what seemed like forever and instead of my mind being clouded by problems it was clear. I got up and went to bed and I fell asleep as soon as my head hit the pillow.

I woke up to the smell of breakfast, so I got up and made my way downstairs and everyone was already up. On my way to the kitchen, I glanced at the clock it was 6:00 a.m. When I went into the kitchen, the twins were helping with breakfast which was a big surprise. Usually, I would have to get them up and it would take them 20 minutes to get it together. Then I thought about when I was their age and would come down here. Being here changed me; it helped me be more responsible, so I see it's doing the same for them. When breakfast was done, we said grace and dug in. We all talked and laughed I thought I needed to come down here to escape. Now I know I needed to be here to be surrounded by love, laughter and family.

After breakfast I got dressed and went out and helped with the day-to-day running of the farm. By the end of the day, I was so tired I took a nap, and I never took naps at home. When I got up, Nana told me that my mother had called so I called her back. She was happy I called. I think she's worried that things will change now that I know the truth, but I flat-out told her she was my mother and that was that.

Nana also said that Chase called, but I didn't call him back. That was the third time he had called since I've been here, but I had avoided his calls. I went and sat on the back porch to think. I had to give this Chase thing some thought, even though I had found out that Jason had been unfaithful with Tee, I still loved him. I know now that I also loved Chase and I don't understand that, plus it makes me feel guilty.

I was sitting there trying to make sense of what I was feeling when Nana came out and sat next to me and told me, "Dinner will be done in a few minutes." I just shook my head and kept on thinking she said, "What's on your mind, Baby?" I wanted to talk to her about it, but I didn't think that she would be able to understand, being that she's only loved one man. I replied, "Nothing, just thinking" Nana wasn't the type to leave someone in deep thought she said, "It must be really deep because you haven't moved from this spot since you came out here."

I told her I was going to call my mother; she would be the right person to go to, plus she needed to be needed. I was so glad Nana understood and I called my mother. She was eager to help, and her advice was good; she told me that the feeling I was having for Chase was normal. He was my first love and if he would've been ready, I probably would have been with him, but he wasn't and that was a part of God's plan. Only God knows what he has planned for us.

She also said take it slow and know that what you're feeling is OK. Don't feel guilty; your heart is where God speaks to you, so just listen. When I hung up, I felt 100% better and I was ready to call Chase.

After dinner I went up to my room and called him. He was happy I called and said he was really worried about me. Plus, he said we needed to talk, and I agreed. To my surprise he asked if he could come down and see me. He said he wanted us to be face-to-face and I said that would be fine. When we hung up, I wondered if Chase coming was a good idea. I went down and talked to my uncle, and he said it was fine and that he could stay in my cousin's old room.

The next day Jada and I dusted the room and got it ready. I don't think Nana was happy to hear that Chase was coming. She didn't say it directly, but the way she was acting let me know but I didn't address it. Two days later Chase arrived, and my uncle and I went to the airport to get him. We were a little late and when we got to the airport Chase had already gotten his luggage and was standing outside. That made my uncle happy, because he was already fussing about paying for parking.

I got out and gave Chase a big hug. Then we got in the truck my uncle looked him up and down and said, "Another pretty boy. I hope you a little more down home than Jason. I loved the boy, but he was like a lost calf down here." Chase smiled and we made our way to the farm. When we got there everyone was already there waiting to see who had come now. They were out back so I showed Chase where his room was, and we headed outside.

Chase brought a few gift bags and gave one to Nana, my uncle and aunt, then the twins. Jada loves presents so she was all smiles, but Lil' Jay just took it and said thanks as he walked away. I made a mental note to get

on his butt about being rude. We all visited while we waited for the food to get done on the grill. I can never get enough of barbecue, so when it was done, I was the first with a plate. We all ate, and all the women were in Chase's face. After we were full, all the men followed my uncle to the garage to smoke and have "man talk" as my uncle called it. That was a nice way to say the men wanted to get out of the way so the ladies could clean up.

When we were done cleaning, I went to the garage to see what they were doing. My cousin John was showing Chase the old school Chevy they were rebuilding. My uncle's garage had everything a real mechanic shop had. He loved working on cars, and said it got his mind off the stress of the farm. I asked Chase if he wanted a tour. I showed him around he said, "When you said farm I thought some small place with a few cows, sheep and stuff but this place is like a small town."

I smiled and said, "Yes, this is a modern farm, and they sell vegetables, cows and milk. My uncle plays broke if you ask him for a loan, but he's very wealthy." He asked, "How long has he had this farm?" I told him, "It's been in our family since 1878. See, this used to be called the Woodlands Plantation when most of my family was brought here from Africa. Then generations of them were born and raised and worked here. The plantation changed hands from son to son, and the last Woodland man was a decent man, and he treated my family very well. He never had any children, so when slavery was over, he kept my family, here, gave them land and paid them to run the plantation. When he died, he left it to my great, great, great grandfather."

"The white folks down here were so pissed that they burned everything down, but they didn't realize who they were messing with because it got rebuilt and rebuilt better than it was before. They went through hell, but they made it and so did the farm. The white folks figured out they weren't going nowhere so they finally just left them alone."

Chase was amazed that this farm had so much history. I took him down on the other side of the pond and I told him that my uncle gave this land to my father to build a house on it. My father only got as far as a design, so I'm using his design and my cousin's construction company will start building in two weeks. I love coming down here, so now when we come, we'll have our own house. And, when it's done, Nana will start coming down here for the winters. She said Minnesota winters and getting to her.

Chase said he loved it here and he would love having a place to go that was so beautiful and peaceful. That was crazy because the only reason I hadn't built the house sooner was Jason: hated coming down here he said it was too quiet. I told Chase when the house was done, he was more than welcome to come down anytime.

We went inside and I could tell Nana was waiting for us because as soon as I told Chase goodnight and he went to his room, she went to bed. I really wanted to talk to her about it, but I knew how she felt. Nana was old school and I think she was concerned that I was spending too much time with Chase.

I was going to go to bed when I heard some movement in the kitchen. I went in and it was my uncle, and he had a chocolate cake. That was strange, because we had carrot cake for dessert. I sat across from him and asked, "Where did you get this cake from?" He smiled and said, "If you promise not to tell, I'll give you a piece." I smiled at him; he was so bad! He was supposed to be on a diet. His doctor told my aunt his sugar was high, and he could develop diabetes if he didn't lose weight. As soon as she heard that she put him on a strict diet. Auntie said, she was already in a wheelchair, and she wasn't going to be his nurse maid. I agreed because that cake was looking to good, plus he said my other aunt had made it. She couldn't cook, but she sure could bake her ass off.

After we ate, I went upstairs and as soon as I opened my door Nana came into the hallway. I gave her this why-are-you-up look, but I really wanted to ask her why she was on guard. I went in the room, and I had to laugh.

I went to bed and when I got up the house was already buzzing. My uncle had decided that he was going to take Chase fishing. Since Auntie's stroke, he hired four more workers. When Nana came, he didn't have the heart to let them go, plus Auntie said he needs to cut back because the stress wasn't good for him, either. With a free day he wanted to go fishing and Chase was all excited. I even talked Lil' Jay into going with them because we were taking Auntie to my cousin Mary Ann's hair shop so we could all get our hair done.

I had to drive because my uncle got a special van for Auntie's wheelchair and Nana didn't like driving it. I was glad because Nana doesn't believe in talking while she's driving; she says it distracts her. When we got there the salon was packed with the usual Saturday clients, plus my cousin Mary Ann's mother (Nana's youngest sister) was there. I loved hanging out with her. She was saved, but let's just say she backslides a lot also you could count on her to piss Nana off. Nana always says that Lilly Mae doesn't have any tact, but I think she just says what's on her mind no matter who it might offend. And, as soon as we settled in there she went.

She came over and put her hand on my shoulder and said, "Umm, umm, umm, Leia. That Chase is something else! If I was a few years younger, child, he might be my new baby daddy." Me and Mary Ann looked

at her, then looked at Nana and laughed. Mary Ann said, "Ma, you need to

stop!" Lilly Mae said, "Child please, I might just snatch him up anyways!

Hell, I need me a little Lovin!" That was all it took, and Nana was on her.

She said, "Lilly Mae Peters, you see this child sitting here. Please watch your

mouth!" Lilly Mae looked at Jada and said to Nana, "Rose, please! This

child ain't no baby. "Then she looked at me, "I know you done had the talk

with that girl, haven't you?" I smiled and said, "Yes, we've had the talk."

Lilly Mae went on, "I know it's only been a few months and all so I

ain't telling you to marry the man, but girl the best way to get over grief is

to get you some!" I took a deep breath because I knew that Nana was about

to snap so I hurried up and tried to change the subject. I walked over to

Auntie and gave her a hair book so she could pick a style. Auntie pulled on

my shirt and waved I knelt down she whispered, "I don't want to choose no

style, child. I'm waiting to see the fireworks. It's been a while since Rose

and Lilly had a good throw down!" I told her we shouldn't let them argue

and she replied, "Girl, please! At my age I try to get my excitement where I

can, and I plan to get it now!"

Lilly Mae said, "Leia, come on over here; don't be trying to be all

secretive about that man." I walked over and said, "I'm not being secretive,

we're friends." She said, "Oh, like they be saying nowadays? Friends with benefits?" I had to laugh, and said, "Now where did you hear that?"

She snapped, "Girl, I ain't that old!" I replied "NO, Auntie, we're just friends, but if it goes any further, you'll be the first to know!" She patted me on my shoulder and said, "OK, now. Don't wait too long. A man as fine as him ain't gone wait too long." That was Nana's breaking point.

She stood up and walked over to her sister and said, "Lilly Mae, Leia and Chase have been friends since they were babies. She just lost her husband, and it is too soon for her to even be thinking about another man, let alone sleeping with him!"

Lilly Mae smirked and said, "Rose, I love and respect you and I ain't trying to call you out, but just cause you gave up on love after Joe passed doesn't mean Leia should do the same. Hell, I loved my husband, too, and no he didn't die. He left me for another woman, but he was gone just the same. I could have just closed my heart to the possibility of love, but I healed my broken heart and moved on. Leia, I know you loved Jason and I know he loved you, but that man wouldn't want you to be alone for the rest of your life!"

This time Mary Ann stepped in to put a stop to the conversation. "Look, both you mean well, and I know Leia appreciates both your opinions, but the last time I checked she was a grown woman with her own mind, so can we please drop it?" After that there was no more talk about Chase.

After we all got our hair done, Mary Ann pulled me aside before we left and suggested that Chase and I go to this new club with her and her boyfriend. I said I would ask Chase if he wanted to go, but I knew he would.

On the way home Nana felt like she had to defend herself. "Leia, I could have dated after Joe passed. I was only in my thirties, but I had a son to raise, plus Joe was all the man I needed. Once he was gone, I was content." I looked at her and I had to tell her so I did "Daddy always wished you would have met someone, because he hated that you were alone. Nana, I've realized through all this that sometimes you must let people go. That doesn't mean you stop loving them, it just means their part in your story is over. Each day I hold on to the love Jason and I shared, but I let him go a bit every day. I will never forget him or the love we shared, but Jason would want me to be happy." She looked at me then touched my hand; I knew she understood what I was trying to say.

When we got home, the guys were already back from fishing. They had cleaned the fish and my cousin Lisa was frying it up. I asked Chase if he wanted to go out with Mary Ann and he said yes. After dinner we got ready, I had brought this brown DKNY halter dress that would be perfect. By the time I got ready Chase was already downstairs waiting with my uncle. When I got downstairs my uncle looked me up and down, as if to see if he approved. Finally, he said I looked beautiful. Then he suggested that we bring a change of clothes because at night the road to the farm was tricky and he didn't want us to get lost or hurt. We brought clothes to stay over at Mary Ann's. I had been down here a lot and I knew these roads, but I've never driven them at night. When we got there Mary Ann and her boyfriend were ready to go, so we made our way to the club.

There was a line around the corner, but lucky for us my cousin's boyfriend had VIP passes, so we didn't have to wait. I was a little shocked, because once we got inside it was nice. It looked like one of the clubs in Downtown Minneapolis. The music was great, and the food was good, there was a huge dance floor which was packed. I think we danced most of the night. I swear I wasn't feeling the four drinks I had. It was four o'clock in the morning by the time we got to Mary Ann's, but I wasn't even tired. Mary Ann's boyfriend John made us all breakfast and it was amazing.

After that I was tired, we went to Mary Ann's guest room and feel right to sleep. The next morning Mary Ann threw me a running outfit and told me to get ready we were going on a run. I was still a little tired, but I didn't think I was going to be able to say no. We ran for almost an hour and when I got back, I went right back to sleep. When I got up Mary Ann said

Nana had called four times so Chase and I made our way back to the farm.

Chapter 12

When we got back to the farm, Nana said she was calling because Sandra had called a few times and that she sounded upset. I took the phone upstairs and called Sandra. "Leia, I'm so glad you called me back. I talked to Alicia, and she told me that you were accusing James of Charles and Jason's murders. What's going on, Leia?"

I sighed and said, "I wanted to talk to you about that myself when I got back. Alicia and I got into it because Chase and I found out a lot of things about James. Sandra, I don't know for sure if he did have anything to do with Jason's murder, but I believe he had something to do with Charles's. Now what role, I don't know, so when Alicia found that out, she called me, and we had words." Sandra replied, "Leia, I trust you and if you believe that James was involved, then by all means find out the truth. But, Baby, you have to be careful because this is our family." I assured her, "I know that Sandra, and that's why I didn't say anything. I wanted to be one hundred percent sure before I said anything to you."

She quickly asked, "Is there anything you'd like me to do to help?" I thought about it for a minute and there was something. James would talk to Sandra if she had the right information to bring to him, so I told her, "You know what, Sandra? There is when I get back. I plan to go see Breanna, so after I speak with her, I want you to talk to James."

She agreed to talk James and after we hung up and I went outside to find Chase. We hadn't talked about the case since he's been here. When I found him, he was playing basketball with Lil' Jay and a few of my cousins so I told him when he was finished, I needed to talk to him. While I waited, I headed to the pond and my auntie was sitting there.

She said, "Hey baby, how is Sandra?" I replied, "Good, how are you?" She answered, "Blessed and definitely favored! When are you going home?" I quickly asked, "Why? Are you trying to get rid of me?" She smiled and said, "No, you know I love having you down here, but not when you're running." I replied, "I am not running, I just needed some time to get my head and heart together." She took my hand and said, "Child, you are running, and you can't run from your problems; they just follow you" I felt the tears forming as I replied, "I am not running from my problems. I'm just putting them on hold for now. When I was at home, I felt like I was drowning."

She wiped the tears that were falling and said, "I know things are hard and what you're dealing with isn't easy, but you have to face it. Hell, look at me. You know how active I was, running around doing this and that, and now, Hell, I can't even get in and out of bed by myself. Sometimes I get so mad, but then I remember what my momma used to say when the shit hit the fan. She said what don't kill you can only make you stronger. So, you have to stand and face it, child. It's just like fighting the devil—you see folks doing it all the time—that's why they all strung up on them drugs or using sex as a release. Baby, you have to face your problems, stand tall with your head held high and tell the problems the same thing you tell the devil…God is bigger than any problems." She was right. I was running and I did have to face them, even if I had to deal with the fact that Breanna, is my real mother. I gave her a big hug and went inside.

I found Chase playing a video game with Lil' Jay. After his turn was over, we went on the back porch to talk. I wanted him to know I was ready to go back and finish what we started. He agreed and we planned to leave on Friday. I told him the first place I wanted to go was to see Breanna. He told me that before he came down here, he had her moved from Shakopee to the county jail and moved her to protective custody so that no one would know where she was. I thought that was good because Breanna was the key to all this. Chase was in a hurry to get back so he could finish his game with Lil' Jay. I sat on the porch for a while longer then went to bed. When I woke up, Nana was in the kitchen making breakfast.

She looked over and said, "I heard you're leaving Friday." I could tell she was worried, so I went over gave her a big hug. I told her I was ready to go home and that everything was going to be fine. She left it alone and I was glad. I had to finish this, whatever the outcome, because I needed all this to be over. I swear the days went by so fast; it was already Thursday. I had butterflies in my stomach all day even though the day was great. They had a big cook out for us, and everyone came. It was so much fun!

By the time I went to bed, I was so tired I didn't remember even falling asleep. When I got up, I rushed to pack and get ready, said my goodbyes and we headed to the airport. The whole way on the plane I just kept telling myself what my auntie had said. What don't kill me can only make me stronger. I felt stronger when we landed, we got our luggage and headed outside just as Nate was pulling up.

We hugged and made our way to my house, and I was surprisingly happy to be home. I went to my room and laid across my bed. Chase came in after an hour or so and said I could go see Breanna in the morning. The rest of the night I was just trying to stay busy so I wouldn't get nervous about seeing Breanna. I took a nice bubble bath to relax and went straight to bed.

I got up and went about getting ready like I was in a trance. On the drive to the jail, I was taking deep breaths, but by the time I was in front of the jail I was hyperventilating. It took me about fifteen minutes to get my breathing normal. Then I got out and went inside and checked in. While I was sitting there, I was thinking about what I was going to say. When they called my name, I felt like running, but when I stood up it was like my legs wouldn't move. I forced myself to walk to the waiting room. I sat down and as soon as I did, Breanna was coming my way. She sat down and I looked at her for a while not speaking just looking at her trying to see if we looked a like and in some ways, we did.

Breanna quickly snapped, "Look, I don't have all day what do you want this time?" I quickly replied, "The truth." She looked at me with this smirk on her face and replied, "And what truth is that?" I said, "The truth about Charles's murder and about you and my father." That smirk was replaced with this serious look. She started to say, "Look, I've told you before..." I stopped her in her tracks. "Don't give me that bullshit about letting sleeping dogs lie, because it's not going to work this time. I know you're my real mother and I also know that you know more than you're saying, so let's put it all on the table." She looked at me, but this time her face had softened, and she had tears in her eyes.

"How did you find out?" she asked. "It really doesn't matter how I found out, I did. Breanna, I know you've been through a lot, and I get that, but you have to understand that I need to do this. I need some closure, so please help me." She looked at me for a minute and then she looked down. I was really hoping she would just do the right thing.

"Leia, I'm so sorry how things turned out… I never meant for you to find out. I met your father at the park; he would go there every day and watch the kids play and I would go to sneak a look at my boys. See, Charles made it seem like I chose to give my boys to Sandra, but I didn't. Charles took them from me the day I left the hospital, but to be honest with you I never wanted to have them. Charles made me, but I loved them.

"Leia, the lifestyle I was living wasn't one I wanted to bring children into, but I want you to know I chose to have you. I would talk to your father, and he wanted a child so bad he would cry. I knew he was filled with so much love and any child would be lucky to have him as a father so I seduced him so I could give him you. I never planned to keep you; it was always my plan to give you to him. Leia, he was the kindest person I had ever met. Most men would just try to sleep with me, but not him. He treated me like a lady. Even after that night he told me he was sorry he never wanted to disrespect me or his wife, so don't judge him harshly. He was a good man."

"Now to Charles, the night he was murdered I was out getting my hair and nails done. When I got home, all the lights were off except for in the basement. I went down because I thought Charles was down there bagging the rocks, but when I got to the top of the steps, I saw Charles's body. As I got closer to the bottom, I saw Allen and James standing there. I ran to Charles and check for a pulse but there wasn't one. Then I jumped up and ran toward them and Allen pulled a gun and told me he would blow my brains out if I moved one more step so I froze."

"Then he said that when the police came, I was going to take the blame, because if I didn't, they were going to go to Sandra's and kill her and my kids. Leia, like I said I didn't want children, but I had them, and they were all I had, so I couldn't let them kill them. So, I took the blame for it. I don't know who pulled the trigger, but they both were there." She was crying and I didn't know what else to do, so I took her hand and held it tight.

"Breanna, thank you for having me. What you did for my mother and father was a blessing, and for that you should feel proud. Not only did you bless them, but you saved your boys and Sandra. There are so many people that only think of themselves, but you didn't, so be proud of that."

She looked at me with tears in her eyes she took my hand and put it to her face "I'm so proud of you; you're so smart and beautiful. When you were little, I would meet your father at the park, and I would watch you play for hours. You were the one thing I had done right! You know when I came here, the only comfort I had was your laughter. I would close my eyes and I could hear you laugh, and it would make me smile. I loved you so much, and I still do." I said, I love you too and I meant it, Breanna made the ultimate sacrifice not once but twice. I didn't love her as a daughter, but as someone who admired her beautiful heart and her strength.

"Thank you, and I look forward to getting to know you." I gave her a big hug, promised her that she would be out soon and then I made my way home. In a way, I was happy that I knew about Breanna; she needs someone, and I planned to be there for her. When I got home, Nate and Chase where both waiting for me. I told them what Breanna told me, then we started brainstorming.

"Leia, I think now is the time to call Sandra and you can go with her when she talks to him. It was one of them that pulled the trigger, and we need to know which one it was." I called Sandra and asked her to call James and ask to see him tomorrow and she agreed. Then I went to see what the guys were doing.

"Nate, have you talked to Alicia?" I asked. "Yeah, but she said that if I ever mention your name, she'll stop seeing me." Nate stopped and then starting talking again" Look I don't know if you two will ever be friends again, but your my family and no one will ever come between that!"

"I don't understand why she is so mad… it's not like I planned this! If she wants to blame someone, she should blame her father." I tried to hold back the tears, but I couldn't. I put my knees to my chest and dropped my head and let it all out. Alicia and I were best friends for 15 years and it hurt that she won't speak to me. Chase came over and sat by me and in a soft voice he tried to comfort me. "Leia, she's probably mad at James but he's her father so she putting her anger on you." I was hoping he was right, but I knew Alicia she was stubborn as hell and when she writes you off there's no making up.

Nate left and Chase and I just sat on the couch. He held me as I drifted off to sleep. When I woke up, Chase was in the shower I went upstairs to wash my face. When I was done, I had to run to catch the phone. It was Sandra. She had spoken with James, and he was coming by at noon, so I told her I would come a little after. I made us some breakfast and then started to get ready.

While I was in the shower, I heard the doorbell. When I got out, I heard Alicia's voice. I put on my robe and went into the hallway. I stood in front of her she looked at me with so much anger. "Look, I don't have shit to say to you, Leia. What you're doing to my father is so wrong!"

"What I'm doing to him, Alicia? Everyone has a choice, and your father chose to be involved in all this. I didn't just put him in it!"

She smirked and said, "Wow, you're really a trip! Let's just say he was there when Charles was killed...so what? Charles was a monster—you even said so yourself. So why should my father go to jail over someone that the world should be glad is dead?"

"Yes, Charles was a horrible person, but Alicia, who were Allen and James to decide if he should have lived or died? You know I feel sorry for what you're going through, but you're mad at the wrong person." She looked at me for a second and then pushed past me and went into the room she had been staying in and started getting her things.

I wasn't about to finish this with her I could see that it wasn't going to end well. So, I just went back in my room and finished getting ready. As I was halfway done, I heard the front door slam. I just finished and went downstairs. Chase asked if I was all right and I told him yes.

It was almost noon, so I made my way to Sandra's. I was a little early, so I parked down the street. When I saw James pull up and go inside, I drove and parked and went inside. James didn't look to happy to see me, but I really didn't expect him to be.

We all sat down, and I took over. "James, I spoke to Breanna, and she told me what really happened that night. Do you want to tell me your side of the story?" He looked at me, then Sandra, and then sat back. But before he could say anything, Sandra sat up in her chair and she said in the loudest voice, "Look at me! I deserve the truth, James. After all these years, tell me the truth!"

He took a deep breath. "I don't know what Breanna said, but yes I was there. Charles had called me and told me to come to the house because he was going to fuck Allen up because he had found out that Allen was stealing. When I got there, Charles and Allen were already in the basement. As I walked through the house, I could hear them fighting and when I got to top of the stairs, I heard the first pop. I ran to the bottom of the steps and Charles was laying on the floor bleeding. Then Allen shot him again."

"No, I didn't stop him, because Charles deserved it. All he had taken from us and how we would hustle our asses off for chump change...Hell, he robbed me of my college education. He took everything from me! He ruined everything he touched, so what he got some rough justice!"

"So, because he was an ass, you all made Breanna suffer for Allen's doing? Look, James, I'm not judging you—see, you have to live with the fact that you watched your brother be murdered, but I do have a problem with you allowing Breanna to take the blame."

He looked at me like I had said something wrong. He stood up and started pointing and waving his hands around. "That bitch wasn't shit but a dope man's whore, so believe me, she didn't have anything to offer the world!"

Sandra stood up and slapped him in the face. "You selfish bastard! She is a person who didn't deserve to spend half her life in prison for you and Allen's sorry asses! Did you help Allen kill my son, and so help me you better tell me the truth because if you don't, you'll never walk out of here!" She bent down and pulled a gun from under the couch I jumped up and took her hand. "Sandra, he's not worth it, I promise you he's not worth it." She looked at me for a minute then she looked at James with tears in her eyes. "You're going to tell me the truth or like I said, they'll be burying your sorry ass!"

James eyes filled with tears then he sat down. "Sandra, I swear on my grandfather I had nothing to do with Jason's death and neither did Allen. If I even thought he did, Allen would be dead." Sandra stood there holding the gun and looking at James and they were eye-to-eye. She put the gun on the table, and I grabbed it and went and put it in her bedroom. When I came back James was walking out, but I had one more question for him.

"Were you there when Tee was killed?" He turned and looked at me and then started out the door. I didn't believe him when he said he walked in on Allen killing Charles…I think he was there the whole time. I also think he was there when Tee was killed, but I didn't think he was there when Jason was killed.

"Leia, do you think he's lying?" Sandra asked. "Yes. He knows Allen killed Jason, and he may not have been there, but he knew. They were trying to keep their secret and I don't care how crazy Charles was—you have to be even more crazy to help someone kill your brother."

"You're right, anyone who is devilish enough to kill his own brother wouldn't think twice about killing his own nephew." Me and Sandra just sat there for a while not saying a word. I think we were both shocked at how James had acted. Nana always said you have to be careful because sometimes the devil comes in all shapes and forms.

I went home and told Chase about what had been said and he agreed with me that James and Allen were both equal in all this. There was one person that could put both James and Allen in Tee's room, and that was Lacey. She was the last piece to this puzzle, and we had to find her. The plan was that I would hit the streets looking and Nate would hit all the strip bars in Minnesota and Chase was going to put a pickup warrant out on her.

A week had gone by, and we weren't any closer to finding her. I was getting
so frustrated.

I had decided to go in the garden to try to relax and after an hour
or so, I was feeling good. I went upstairs when I heard someone beating on
the front door. I swear I thought they were going to knock it down! I
looked out the peep hole and it was Frank, Chase's partner. I opened the
door too fast because I was about to let his ass have it knocking on my
door like he was crazy. But I didn't get a chance to say anything because he
just rushed past me and started looking around then he grabbed my hand.

"We have to go! Chase has been shot!" It felt like someone had hit
me in the chest and I couldn't move. Frank was pulling me, but I just
couldn't move so he stopped. "Leia, he's all right. I'll tell you what
happened on the way to the hospital. Once I knew Chase was OK, I
grabbed my purse, locked the door and we headed to the hospital.

On the way, Frank began telling me what happened. He said that
someone called him and wanted to meet him because they had information
on the Richardson case. So, he went to a parking lot off Cedar Avenue in
Minneapolis, he said he got out the car he saw a truck coming toward him.
Instead of stopping, it rode past, and the window was cracked. Then he said
he heard the shots. One hit his bulletproof vest the other hit him in the
shoulder."

"Did he get the license plate number?" I asked. "There were no plates, and the windows were tinted, so we don't hold out any hope finding it."

When we got to the hospital I went straight to Chase's room and his mother was there sitting by his bedside. She looked up and waved for me to stop and she came over to me. We went into the hall. "I'm sorry, I just didn't want you to wake him. He just fell asleep."

"That's fine I'm just glad he's all right," I said. "Me too, I hope this makes him see that he needs to take the bar and leave the force." I agreed, "I hope he does, too. I just don't understand why he won't take the bar." She replied, "Honestly, Leia, I think that he's doing this to piss Allen off."

"Why would Allen be mad that Chase was on the force? I'd think he would be proud," She looked at me and laughed. "Come on, let's go to the cafeteria and get some coffee." We went downstairs to the cafeteria got some coffee and went and found a seat by the window.

"Leia, Allen hates that Chase is a detective. See, even though Allen stopped hustling he still considers himself a thug...what a joke. When Chase joined the force instead of taking the bar, Allen hit the roof. He went on and on about how he wasn't going to have —excuse my language—but no fuckin cops in his family. When he saw that he couldn't stop Chase, he just wrote him off, which was fine by Chase. I know this sounds so bad, but

I'm so glad that Chase doesn't like his father; that was the only comfort I had while Chase was growing up. At least I knew that Chase would go out of his way to not be like Allen."

"No, it's not bad, I know how you feel. I would look at Lil' Jay and just pray that he doesn't end up hustling, but the one thing that I have in my favor was Jason. He went out of his way to talk to Lil' Jay and let him know that he didn't want that for him. He really didn't. He wanted Lil' Jay to go to college and be something, and I know he will." We sat there for a while longer and talked, then we went back to the room, Chase was awake.

"I was wondering where you two were," he said. "We went to get coffee and didn't want to wake you," I said. He smiled at me, and I was so happy that he was all right. His mother left for a while; she said she had to change, and she would be back. Before she left, she winked at me and said, "I'm trusting you to take care of my baby." I smiled and winked back. I really liked her. She really loves Chase, and he adores her. I was kind of glad she left so I could get some information about what happened.

I asked, "Do you think it was Allen and James?" He said, "You know, I've been laying here thinking about that and I think there's someone helping them because I can't see either one of them getting their hands dirty at this point."

I thought about it and said, "I think you're right; I just can't think of who it could be. I'll have Nate check and see if there are any new faces around them." Just then, Nate came through the door. "Man, I thought you was dead! Shit, word on the street is that you got smoked!" Chase laughed, "Damn, shit travels fast. But nope, I'm not dead, but they sure did try!" Nate laughed "Man, this shit is deep. I've been watching my back all day,"

Chase handed Nate his house keys. "That's good...don't get caught slipping. Look, go to my crib and look in my hall closet and get a vest." "Man, I'm a rider I ain't wearing no vest. If my number's up, it's up!"

"Nate, I know how you feel, but please wear one for me. You're like my brother and I swear I would lose it if something happened to you, so please for me and the kids." He looked at me and I gave him my sad face and he took the keys. "Baby girl, I'll do anything for you and the kids," and gave me a big hug.

"Oh shit, you'll almost made me forget about my good news! I found Lacey! I went to this strip joint in Hudson and this chick said Lacey had been dancing there for a few weeks and then she bounced to Vegas with this other chick. She even knew the name of the club they went to and I called and sure as shit stank, they were there."

I was so happy! Now all we had to do was get her. Chase called his boss and had him call Vegas PD to have her picked up. We sat there all quiet, waiting for Chase's boss to call back. It seemed like hours. Mary was back and she was trying to figure out what was going on.

When the phone rang, we all jumped Chase got it and said, "Yes, OK, thank you." Then he gave us the best news: The Vegas PD had Lacey in custody and would be sending her back tomorrow. Chase got the number to the detective that took her in and gave him strict instructions. He told him to let her make her one phone call but to have it monitored. He wanted to know who she called and what was said. Chase was hoping she would call James or Allen.

Chase had dinner and we still hadn't heard back from the detective. So, me, Mary and Nate decided to go get some food. We went to this place by the hospital and got some take out and went back to the room. "I got the call, and you'll never guess who she called and what was said!" I was sure it was James. "Who, James?" He said, "Nope, your brother!"

Well, I wasn't that surprised, because we knew they were messing around. Maybe she thought he would bail her out. "What, was she begging him to get her out?" He said, "Oh no, she was snapping. She said she wasn't going to go down for their bullshit and he better find a way to get her out of this mess." I was so confused. What mess was she talking about? Then it hit me like a ton of bricks: Lance was somehow involved in all this. "I knew Lance was a creep, but a murder"

"Leia, I don't know if he killed anyone, but I promise you I plan to find out." We all sat there pondering it all, then Nate left, and Mary and I settled in for the night on the couch in Chase's room.

Chapter 13

The next morning, Frank came and told Chase he would do all his legwork. Chase told him to follow Lance, because he wanted to know his every move. Chase called his old patrol partner; he said he was the only one he trusted to go to the airport to get Lacey. He said John was the only white boy he trusted, so when he got to the hospital Chase was very serious.

"John, this shit is deep, so you have to watch your ass. They might try to take her out because she's the only person that can tie them all together," he explained. John laughed and said "Damn, Chase! The first time you call me for a favor it has to involve my risking my life!" he smiled then he rubbed his head. "Well shit, you know I'm not all there upstairs, so this is the shit that gets my heart racing. I just don't understand Why them dumb fucks let her live, anyways? You'd think they would've gotten rid of her ass!"

"Man, I've been trying to figure that one out myself, but we'll have all the answer as soon as you bring her in."

John left and again and we waited. I swear I was so nervous I went down to the chapel and said a prayer for John. I was really hoping they didn't try anything; Chase said they probably wouldn't, but at this point we couldn't put anything past them. When I got back to the room Chase said he talked to Frank, and Lance went to James's shop, and it looked like the two were arguing about something. Then they both got into Lance's car and went to my dad's office and they're all there right now. So, it was official... Lance was a part of this.

"Chase, I swear if it was Lance that killed Jason, so help me!" Chase stopped me before I could finish my sentence. "Leia, just let it go. He wouldn't be worth it." He was right. Lance wasn't worth it, but I really can't believe this—all that he has done, now this? I wanted to call my mother, but I knew this would break her heart. If Lance was somehow involved in this, she would find out soon enough but I wanted to wait as long as possible to tell her.

Chase called his office and told his boss he didn't want anyone to talk to her; that he wanted to do it himself. When he got off the phone, me and his mother were staring him down. "What's wrong with you two?"

"Chase Anthony Thompson, you aren't going anywhere. The doctors said you need to rest!" He replied, "Mom I'll rest when those guys are behind bars." I sided with his mom, saying, "Chase, your mother's right. I want them as bad as you do, but I don't want you to risk your health to get them." I knew he wasn't listening because as I was talking, he was getting dressed.

"As long as they're out there we all are in danger, so the sooner we get them the better." Chase got dressed and his mother and I drove him to the station. He made us wait in the front while he got Lacey sent to an interrogation room. He came back and got me and said I could listen from behind the double glass. I was so nervous, and I didn't know why. This was the moment I had been waiting for. Chase walked in and Lacey rolled her eyes and started playing with her nails. Chase sat down across from her.

"Would you like something to drink?" he offered. "Sure, you got a shot of vodka?" Then she laughed and continued to play with her nails.

"Nope, all I have is some coffee or water." When she said, "Then I'll pass," I was thinking they should cut the chitchat, and get to it already. Chase

"Lacey, you weren't honest with us about Tee's murder, were you?" he began. "I have no idea what you're talking about I told you everything that happened" She never looked up she just kept picking at her nails.

"Look Lacey, you can play this tough shit if you want to, but I have a witness that puts you in the room when Tee was killed, so it would be in your best interest to cooperate."

She laughed and looked at Chase, "You most think I'm some kind of fool. I may be a stripper, but I ain't dumb." She rolled her eyes again and kept picking at her chipped acrylic nails.

Chase didn't say a word; he just got up and went out of the room. I thought damn, Chase, you're giving up too easy. Then he came back with an officer, closed the door and stood by the chair where he was sitting.

"Lacey, can you please stand?" Lacey looked at him and reluctantly stood up. The officer walked behind her, and she looked back at him. "Lacey, please place your hands behind your back." She looked puzzled, then she did what he asked. "You have the right to remain silent..." Lacey shouted so loudly the glass shook. "What in the hell are you doing? They already read me my rights!" Chase looked at her and said, "Yes, that was when you were being held, but now you're being charged with conspiracy to commit murder. You have the right to..."

Lacey interrupted again, "Wait, just a minute! How are you going to charge me with conspiracy to commit murder?"

"Like I told you, I have a witness that puts you in the room when Tee was killed," Chase replied. I guess Lacey thought that Chase was

241

bluffing about the witness, but he continued to read her rights and she was taken back to her cell.

I meet him in the front and asked, "Chase, what was that? She didn't even tell you anything."

He replied, "Leia, this isn't TV. What, did you think she was going to confess? Sometimes it takes a day or two.

We took his mother home then we went to Frank's. Chase said it wasn't safe for us to go back to our houses, plus he said Frank was always at his girlfriend's house. When we got there, I was really not impressed. Frank lived in a tiny one bedroom. I walked in and was trying to figure out where I was going to sit. "Frank really needs to invest in a housekeeper," I said. "Yeah, not on his salary." I said, "Look at your place—it's nice." He said, "Well, I don't have an ex-wife and child to support, plus I have money from my weed days, and you know my grandfather left me a lot of money." I laughed, "Um, so you're loaded? Let me snatch you up now!" We both laughed and chase cleaned up because I wasn't touching anything. We ordered a pizza and watched some TV.

"Chase, so I heard you joined the force to piss your father off." He looked at me and smiled. "I wonder were you heard that from? But I guess I did. One day he was talking about how he had gotten pulled over for no reason and how if you were black and in a nice car you were a target for Saint Paul's finest."

"Well, Chase he was right. Being black in Minnesota is enough to get you pulled over, detained or just downright harassed by the police. It used to happen to my dad all the time." He said, "I know, Leia, I happen to be black. Even though I'm a detective, if I'm out of my area I get the same thing. That's one of the things I hate about living here. That shit sucks but knowing that my dad hated the police was enough for me. I plan to take the bar but I have respect for the good cops who don't see race, but there are more racist assholes than good cops."

I was so glad he was going to quit, because seeing him in the hospital really scared me and I didn't want to lose him. I didn't know what the future had in store, but I wanted him in it.

We woke up to the phone ringing. It was Frank. He told Chase that Lacey had thrown up all night, so she was taken to the hospital. They found out that she was four and a half months pregnant. Chase said that must have been why they didn't kill her—she was pregnant, and he was almost certain that it was Lance's baby. Wow, that was a scary thought; another weirdo running around was not good. Chase said that was good to know, because when he went to talk to her tomorrow that he would play on that. I was wondering why he wanted to wait until tomorrow to talk to her, but I didn't ask. I figured that Chase knew what he was doing, and I trusted his judgment. Plus, it was good that he was staying in because he needed the rest.

I gave Chase his pain pills after breakfast, and he was asleep an hour later. I was really bored at Frank's, so I called Nate and he picked me up. I wanted to shop—I hadn't shopped in forever and I was really missing my favorite store. Dayton's was like a second home to me. I told Nate about Lacey and he couldn't believe that she was pregnant by Lance.

"I swear Leia, I thought that dude was gay," he said. "Why did you think that?" I asked. "Leia, I never told you this, but when Jason had his second birthday party last year, Lance was tripping. He got drunk and all he was talking about was how Jason was so good looking and how he dressed, and all kinds of weird shit. I told Jason he better watch him!"

I remembered that I was pissed when I found out because he had it at this strip bar in Downtown Minneapolis, but I didn't know Jason invited Lance. It didn't surprise me, though. He was always trying to get me to hang out with Lance. He said Lance was my brother and I should make an effort to get along with him. I never really told Jason how I felt about Lance; I guess I felt a little ashamed of it. I was taught to treat everyone with respect and not to hate anything or anyone.

"His ass is probably bisexual. You know that stuff's going around. I read an article about these homo thugs!" Nate looked at me like I was crazy. "Homo what?" I explained, "Homo thugs. Brothers who are like gangsters running around packing nines and banging in the streets but ultimate freaks under the sheets."

"Man, you're buggin!" I said, "No really, they are all hardcore but then they sneak around gay bars in the dark, so you better watch your homies." He looked at me and shook his head, "That's some crazy shit! Man, what the fuck is wrong with brothers nowadays when getting some pussy isn't enough?"

"Nathaniel Butler, watch your mouth," I said. "I'm sorry, but that shit is freaking me out. You not only got to watch your back for haters, but now you got to watch yo ass from your homies!" I laughed. Nate was a fool, but he was right.

I walked around the store looking at these hot jeans...I was definitely getting a pair. I looked up to see where Nate was when I saw one of my old professors. Oh shit, I tried to hide behind the rack, but he saw me.

"Leia Richardson, I have been trying to reach you ever since the graduation. Why didn't you show up? You were going to be given an award—you were in the top five in your field!" I knew my grades were perfect, but I didn't think I was in the top five! I gave myself a little pat on the back. "I'm so sorry, Professor Peterson but I lost my husband earlier this summer and I took it really hard." He grabbed me and gave me a big hug.

"Why in the world didn't you call me?" I guess I really should have. He was the best professor I ever had, and he was a great person. Being in a state that is predominantly white was hard and being in a college with more whites than blacks was even harder. Most professors assumed that I wasn't smart, that I was just there to fill a quota. I would get so mad and one day he told me not to ever give up and not to let those racist buttheads get to me. He said they were just mad because I was smart and that intimidated them. It was a shame that we have come so far as a nation, but we still have people like that to deal with. He really made my life at college bearable.

"I'm sorry it's just been hard," I explained. He smiled "Well, you have my number and please don't hesitate to use it. I mean it, day or night, OK?" I agreed and we went our separate ways. It really was good to see him and after all this, I really may take him up on his offer. I continued to shop but made a note to stop by the house to get my messages.

I didn't even check my answering machine when I got back, plus I hadn't gotten around to going to my neighbor Marie's to get my mail. When I got to the house, I saw Alicia's car in the driveway. I was hoping that she had changed her mind and come to apologize but I knew that wasn't going

to be the case. Nate hurried to say he'd wait in the car, so I went to Marie's,

got the mail then took a deep breath and went inside the house. Alicia was

sitting on the couch flipping through a magazine. I sat down in the chair

across from her. She looked up at me with no emotion.

"I wanted to talk to you. I spoke with my father, and he told me

what he told you and Sandra. I know that he probably made the wrong

decision helping Allen, but after what Charles did to him how could you

blame him? Leia I am asking you to leave my father out of this. He has to

deal with what he did, but I know beyond a shadow of a doubt that he had

nothing to do with Jason's murder." After she was finished, I looked at her,

but this time she was very emotional and had tears in her eyes. I wish I

could tell her what she wanted to hear, but I couldn't.

"I truly understand were you're coming from, Alicia. If I could, I

really wouldn't include James, but it's not that simple. He was there and

whether or not he pulled the trigger is for a jury to decide." Before I could

finish Alicia was standing in front of me looking at me like she wanted to

knock me out. I sat back in my chair and looked her eye-to-eye to let her

know I wasn't going to back down.

"Leia, you know what? I used to think of you as a sister but now I

don't plan to think of you at all." She walked to the door and turned and looked at me and said, "You have a nice life." Then she walked out. That

was very hard; I love her more then she'll ever know and if it had been

anyone else, I wouldn't have pressed the issue.

No matter what kind of person Charles was, he was Jason's father

and he died trying to find out the truth. I planned to see that the truth came

out. I listened to the messages, grabbed a few things, then headed back to

Frank's. The whole way there I fought back the tears. Alicia was the closest

thing I had to a sister, and now I knew for sure she wasn't going to be in

my life anymore. That was a hard pill to swallow.

Chapter 14

I woke up and Chase was already getting ready. I said good morning and started getting ready too. I think we were both anxious. It usually took me an hour in a half or so to get ready and that was only if I was in a hurry. Not today… it took me thirty minutes and we were on our way. The whole way there I was praying that Lacey would tell Chase the truth about what happened. I was so ready to have all this behind me.

When we got to the station Chase sent for Lacey and I waited in the lobby until she was brought to an interrogation room. Chase came and got me and again I waited on the other side of the double glass, but this time Frank was in there with me. We watched as Lacey sat there looking uncomfortable; she kept moving around in her chair. Then she grabbed the waste basket and threw up. Chase walked in carrying a hand full of stuff he handed her a 7UP. "Thank you, they wouldn't give me any pop downstairs."

"I know. I also have some crackers for you." He handed her a pack of saltine crackers she smiled and grabbed them and ate about ten in a row. "Are you feeling better?" he asked? "Yes, thank you."

"Look, Lacey you're pregnant. Do you really want to have your baby inside?" She looked at him and then at her stomach. "It's not that easy. I have a lot to lose if I talk."

"You'll lose more if you don't. Not only will you have that baby inside, but you'll lose custody of it. Do you want your child to get adopted, or worse raised in foster care?" Her face turned red and then she started to cry. "I don't want my baby in foster care That's why I'm so screwed up; being bounced from home-to-home running when the abuse starts or fighting off perverts! I don't want that for my child!"

"Then give it a chance. Tell me what I need to know, and I'll promise you a lovely deal that won't have any jail time." She put her hand on her stomach and looked down at it as if she was trying to really focus on what was best for her baby.

"If I tell you then my baby won't have a father and then what are we supposed to do?"

"If you talk your baby will have more a loving family a grandmother and the best aunt in the world," he said. She looked up at him and made a face. "Do you really think those stuck-up people will have anything to do with me or my baby? Please. Lance told me how uppity they are."

"Look, the two options are this: jail or freedom. Now what are you going to choose?" I think that did it. She touched her stomach and Chase turned on the tape recorder and then began with his questions.

"Were you in the room when Tanisha Jackson was murdered?"

She looked down and whispered," Yes."

"I need you to speak loudly and clearly."

"Yes, I was there."

"Who else was there with you?"

"Lance and Allen and me"

For the record, could you state their last names?"

"Lance Wilson and Allen Thompson."

"Thank you. Now I'll need you to tell me what happened." She looked up at the ceiling and then she moved around in her chair a little then she began the story:

"After I had spoken to Leia, I called Lance and told him that she was looking for Tee. He told me to meet him at the motel the next day. I waited in my car until he pulled up and he had Allen with him. They hid on the side of the door, and I knocked. Tee opened the door and when she did, they pushed their way in. Once we were inside, they started to beat her up. Then they took her into the bathroom, and they were in there for about 15 minutes and then I heard a muted bang, and they came out. Allen told me what to say to the police and to you guys. He said if I fucked up, I was going to be next."

"Do you know who shot her?"

"No, like I said they went into the bathroom."

"Did you know that they were going to kill her?"

"No, I was shocked when they started to beat her."

"Why were you shocked? You knew she was hiding from Them"

"No, she was hiding from you guys. After Jason was killed, Tee got really scared and she knew that she was next, so she was trying to come up with a plan. All she kept saying was that she had to find a way to get to them and make a deal." I felt sick once I heard that. She was trying to make a deal with Jason's killer.

"you're saying that Tanisha was trying to make a deal with

Allen to spare her life"

"Yes, Tee said she had something to bargain with."

"So, it was Allen who killed Jason?"

She looked down and then she looked at Chase "No, Lance

Did."

"Why would Lance kill Jason?"

"He works for Allen and he does whatever Allen tells him

To do/"

"To your knowledge, did James know of any of this?"

"No, Lance told me that James didn't know he killed Jason or Tee. James didn't even know Lance worked for Allen. Also, Lance told me that Allen told him to keep an eye on James because he might be the next to be taken out."

I stood there with tears rolling down my face. I couldn't believe it. Lance killed Jason. I knew he hated me, but I would have never thought he was the one who killed Jason. Frank came over and put his arm around me and I laid my head on his shoulder as we finished listening to Lacey's story.

"Look, I know you think I'm a gangster groupie, but I'm not. I turn tricks from time to time if the money's right and Lance's money was right. I would see him twice a week. I want more out of life. I want to go to college and getting pregnant by Lance was my ticket to a better life." Chase interrupted Lacey, "I'm not judging you, Lacey. What you do with your life is your business; I'm here to find Jason's killer, that's it."

"Well, on the day Jason was killed Lance called me. I met him at a motel and when I got in the room, I could tell something was wrong. He was sweating and pacing back and forth. I was about to leave when he grabbed me by the arm and started crying. I didn't know what to do…I was scared, and I didn't know what was going on. He sat me on the bed and pulled out a gun and started waving it around. I grabbed his hand, talked to him slowly and calmly—I was just trying to make it out of there alive."

"Lance told me that he had done something really bad, and he had to tell someone. I was the only one he could tell, and if I told someone he would kill me and the baby. He told me he killed Jason. I only knew one Jason and that was Tee's best friend. I swear I didn't even know Lance was Leia's half-brother!"

"I stayed with him the rest of the night and I went to Tee's after I left him. When I got there, she was a mess. She said she had just come back from the hospital with Leia and Jason's mom. I was scared of Lance, but I loved Tee. I told her what Lance had told me and she was mad at first. Then she told me she was pregnant, and she couldn't risk the life of her child, so she asked me to set up a meeting with Lance. I did and they made a deal, so when they killed her, I was shocked and scared."

"Did he say why he killed Jason?" Chase asked. Lacey replied, "He said that Allen paid him $15,000 to kill Jason."

He killed my husband for $15,000! I was angry! Lance's father was very wealthy and gives him whatever he wants. I knew he didn't kill Jason for money; he didn't need to. I wanted to go find him and do to him what he did to Jason.

Chase asked her few more questions and then he came into the room. He took my hand and said, "Leia, I'm so sorry I know this is really hard." He was wrong... it was more than hard. It was a nightmare. I asked, "What happens now?"

"I'll issue warrants for my dad, Lance and James. I want you to go to Frank's and I'll call you when they've been picked up." I said, "I want to go to my mom's; I need to tell her all this. I don't want her to hear it on the news or in the paper." He agreed and Frank took me to my mother's house. I was glad she was home. When I went inside, she was sitting at the kitchen table paying her bills. I kissed her on the forehead and sat down across from her and she smiled at me. I swear I didn't want to tell her, but I know she had to know.

"Mom, I have something to tell you and I just want you to know none of this is your fault. I know you blame yourself for Lance's behavior, but he is a grown man and no matter who his father is, he knows right from wrong. He chose to be the kind of person that he is, and you can't blame yourself for that, nor can you beat yourself up for leaving him behind."

Her smile was replaced with confusion. "Leia, what has Lance done now? Just tell me." I reached across the table and took her hand. "Lance was the one who killed Jason and was also there when Tee was killed. I don't know yet if it was him or Allen who killed her, but we'll soon find that out." She slid her hand from under mine and she got up and went into her room. I followed her and I sat on the bed next to her and rubbed her back. "Mom, I'm so sorry! The last thing I wanted to do was see you in pain."

She lifted her head up and tried to smile but it wouldn't form. "I heard what you said, but Leia the man he turned out to be is my fault. If I would've stayed or tried harder to get him, he wouldn't have been so angry and none of this would have happened!" She dropped her head back on the bed and began to cry again.

"I know you think that, but it's not true. Daddy always told me that God gives us all free will to live our lives the way we choose. Some people choose to live right and do good things and then there are people who choose to do bad things. It's their free will and someday we all have to stand in front of God and answer for what we've done. No matter who Lance was raised by or what his environment was, he has free will and he choose to be the person he is. He could have embraced you and I and we could have been a happy family, but instead he choose to hold a grudge and that grudge is what festered in him and turned him into a murderer. Mom, it's time to forgive yourself for everything, especially for the things you can't change. Don't let the guilt fester inside you...let it go. Me and the kids need you and your new grandchild needs you." She looked up at me and wiped her tears away. "You're pregnant?"

"No, but Lance has a baby on the way, and from the looks of it, the mother needs a lot of support." I knew it was a lot to take in, so I kissed her and let her take a nap.

I went into her office and called Nana and filled her in on what was going on. She said she wasn't a bit surprised—she knew that Lance was evil. I told her I had to call Sandra and I would call after everything was over.

I called Sandra next and told her what happened. She wanted to come over and sit with us while we waited. I kept picking up the phone and checking the line and looking at my cell to see if it was on. I was pacing and going crazy by the time Sandra got there. We decided to make something to eat to get our minds off everything. By the time the food was done, my mom had gotten up and joined us in the kitchen. We were about to eat when the phone rang. We all stopped and looked at each other, then it rang again, and I went and picked it up.

Chase was on the other end and when I heard his voice my heart started beating fast. He said that his father and James had been picked up, but there was a problem when they tried to pick up Lance. He said that Lance wasn't home when they got there, but he pulled up as the officers were leaving. There was a chase, but Lance got away. He told me to make sure the doors were locked, and he'd be here as soon as he could. I hung up the phone and went to check the front door and it was locked. I was hoping that Chase would get here soon because I didn't feel safe with Lance on the loose.

Chapter 15

After we ate and cleaned up, we sat in the living room trying to relax and not think about what was going on. When the doorbell rang, I looked through the peephole and saw Chase. I opened the door and gave him a big hug; I was so glad to see him. He came in and we all sat down. We all wanted to hear what happened when Allen and James were brought in. We all started asking questions at the same time.

"What did they say, Chase? I need to know why they did this to Jason!"

"My father isn't talking, and neither is James. They both lawyered up, so now it's a waiting game to see who wants a deal first."

"How long do you think it will take to catch Lance?"

"I'm not sure, Sandra. All the cops on patrol have been notified to look out for him, so I hope very soon."

Chase wanted us all to stay together until Lance was brought in. He said that Lance might try to hurt me or my mom, so we went back to my house. Chase stayed with us and there were two unmarked cars outside so I felt safe, but that whole night I couldn't sleep I kept tossing and turning. I was awakened by the phone—it was Chase's partner. I went into the guest room and gave Chase the phone and stood there listening, hoping it was news about Lance.

"Did they catch him, Chase?" He waved for me to wait and then when he got off the phone, he started grabbing his clothes.

"So, are you going to tell me or what?" He was still putting on his clothes.

"Get your mom up and tell her we need to leave now."

"What's going on?"

"Leia, I'll tell you in the car! Please get your mom!"

I was going to push but he had a serious look, so I went and told mom to get dressed because we needed to leave. She was asking me the same questions I was asking Chase, but I didn't have any answers. I rushed and got dressed and went downstairs and I was shocked to see Chase waiting in the car for us. I yelled up to my mom to hurry up. I wanted to know what this was all about.

When we got in the car, Chase was on his cell again, which meant I would have to wait. I swear I was about to snatch that phone, but then I realized he was talking to his mother. When he hung up, he took a deep breath.

"Is she all, right?"

"Yes, she's fine. I wanted to see if my father had tried to call her."

"Did he?"

"Nope, and she said she's glad he didn't."

"Now can you tell me what's going on?"

"Frank said James asked to see me so I think he's ready to talk."

I took a deep breath. I guess I knew that at some point we would have to hear what James's involvement was, but now I wasn't prepared for it. When we got to the jail, Chase told us that we could watch the interrogation from the double glass. My mother said she really didn't want to, so Chase told her she could sit at his desk.

When we got inside the station, I saw Alicia and her mother sitting on the bench in front of the main desk. As we walked past, Rhonda grabbed my hand and stood up. "Leia, I'm not mad at you. You did what was right and hopefully someday Alicia will see that." She gave me a big hug and whispered in my ear, "I'm sorry." I took her hand and said, "Rhonda, you don't have anything to be sorry about." Then I looked at Alicia and she turned her head, so I just followed Chase.

He took my mother to his desk then we went to the interrogation room he put me in the other room. This time Frank and the chief were in there with me. I saw James sitting there in his blue jailhouse clothes and I wanted to cry. Chase walked in and sat down in front of James.

"Do you want anything to drink before we start?"

James shook his head no and said, "I just want to get this shit off my chest. I've been carrying it around for 30 plus years."

"Well, you can start wherever you'd like."

James took a deep breath and began to speak. "When I moved to Minnesota all I wanted to do was go to college and be close to my brother, but things didn't work out that way. First, I lost my scholarship, then somehow, I got into the dope game. After they took my scholarship, I was going to go back home, but Charles said he wanted me to stay. He said he didn't have anyone he could trust to watch his back. I hesitated at first, but Charles really laid it on thick… made like he needed me. I really wanted us to be close, so I finally gave in."

"Unfortunately, I learned sooner than later that he was on bullshit. All he really wanted was to fuck up my life, which he tried his best to do. For two months, I watched one of his spots, then out of the blue he decided that I had to hit the streets. I tried to tell him I wasn't cut out for it—hell, I was a church boy—I hadn't even smoked herb until I got to Minnesota, but Charles didn't care. He said, "Hit the streets!" and me trying to be a good brother, I did."

"Two weeks later, I was robbed and shot. To make matters worse, once I got out of the hospital, Charles beat the shit out of me. Told he was making me tough. Shit, I was a damn fool! I should have left then, but I again, I wanted to be a good brother. Man, Charles treated me like the dirt under his shoe, but I guess I wanted to believe that deep down he loved me. He had to… I was his brother." James stopped and tears started to roll down his face. Chase sat back I felt so bad for James. Chase stood up and told James he would give him a minute to get it together and he walked out.

I meet Chase at the door, he asked me to go back inside. I sat down knowing he had something on his mind.

"Leia, I know deep down you want James just to be guilty of knowing about Charles's murder, but I've been doing this for a while, and I think it's deeper than that." I knew what he was saying, but I hadn't rushed to judgment this far, so I was going to wait it out and hear his whole story. "Chase, I know there is a chance that James had something to do with Jason's murder, but good or bad I want to hear it from him." Chase looked at me and went back into the interview room.

263

I took a deep breath and turned to the two-way window. Chase sat down and James had his head down. He slowly lifted his head and looked at Chase, and before Chase could say another word, James started where he left off. "I put up with his shit; we all did, and we watched that dude do some crazy shit to people. Man, one day this kid name Remo stole some dope from one of Charles's dealers and Charles went crazy. He said he had to show people that he wasn't the one to fuck with. He found Remo, took him in his basement put on a big pot of cooking oil and stuck that boy's arms in it."

"Then there was this one cat that ran for Charles who got caught up. It was his fault he was hanging on the corner shooting dice when five-o ran up on him. He ran and had to throw two zips and Charles went crazy. It was to the basement... the fool beat that boy so bad I thought he was going to kill him. Then all of a sudden, he stopped, went upstairs and came back with this huge bottle of alcohol. Charles bent down snatched his shit off and poured that stuff all over him. Man, I've never heard anyone scream like that in my life and I hope I never do again. That cat was eighteen. He died on that basement floor."

James stood up and rubbed his hands over his head and paced back and forth around the room Chase just watched him. "James, look I know you've been through a lot, but I really need to speed this up." James looked at him and then sat down. "I'm getting there but I need you to know the whole true about Charles to understand why I did what I did." Chase looked at James. I think he knew that he needed to cleanse his soul.

"When I was young, I would sit in the pews and listen to my grandfather talk about people being possessed by demons, and I always thought it was to scare all the kids into being good. I changed my mind once I saw the things Charles did to people. I know you heard about that one dude Aaron Wright." Chase sat up and looked at James. "Yeah, who hasn't? The shit that happened to him was crazy…don't tell me Charles did that?" James looked at Chase and said, "Chase he tortured that man for four days in that basement. They cut off his fingers knocked out all of his teeth, burned him with cigarettes and the last day they took him down by the Mississippi River and set him on fire."

"Who helped Charles?"

James looked down then up at Chase as if he didn't want to answer, but I think Chase already knew who he was going to say. "Your father."

"Why did they do that to him? From what I understand he was a square, worked 12-hour days at the Ford Plant and never bothered anyone. That's why they never solve his case…no one could figure out who would want to hurt him," Chase said.

"It was over Brianna. She was getting tired of Charles's shit. After she disappeared and came back, she was different. She kept talking about wanting more out of life and that she didn't want to be in the game anymore. Charles was fighting her more, and plus the whole thing with Sandra. She was just tired. I guess she started fooling around with Aaron and he really loved Brianna. She wanted him to run away with her, but I guess Aaron felt like why they should run Charles would have to understand that she didn't want to be with him anymore. He didn't know Charles, but Brianna did, that's why she wanted to run."

"One day while Brianna was gone, he showed up to the house to have a man-to-man with Charles, but he never left. Brianna came home and Charles beat her up and dragged her to the basement. For the next four days, she had to watch Charles torture the man she loved." I was in tears. I couldn't imagine what she must have felt; how scared she was, and she had no one to turn to.

"James, why would my father help him kill Aaron? What was in it for him?" James looked at Chase for a minute, like he really didn't want to go there. "Chase, there is a lot you don't know about your father, and I really don't think you want to know." Chase replied, "James I know you're trying to somehow spare me, but I want you to know that I hate Allen, so there's nothing you can say that would bother me."

"All right then, you want to know what was in it for your father? Nothing. See, your father was just as evil as Charles was and got a kick out of doing that crazy shit. He would look for reasons for him and Charles to do some sick shit to someone. He loved every minute of it, plus he wanted him and Charles to be best friends. I guess he was like me in a way, trying so hard to get in Charles's good graces. The only difference was I wasn't willing to sell my soul to the devil to get Charles's love. But Allen was."

"It wasn't until your father found out that your mom had been with Charles that things changed. Allen was angry and he didn't want revenge... he wanted to see Charles dead. He asked me over and over to help him, and again and again I told him no. Charles was evil and on some level by that point, I didn't like him very much. But he was still my brother."

"It wasn't until Allen told me something that would change my life forever. You see my grandfather was robbed and killed leaving his church one night. I was crushed and as soon as I found out, I called Charles out in Vegas. He met me in Chicago, stayed by my side the whole time, acted like he was sad for me. He even cried at the funeral. After that, Allen told me Charles was the one who killed our grandfather. I couldn't believe it."

"I knew Charles was a monster, but to do that he would have to be Satan himself. He told me that Charles talked about killing granddad since he was a kid, because he hated my grandfather for not taking him in. I drove myself crazy for three days. There was a part of me that wanted to know for sure that Charles did it, but there was another part that didn't. When my grandfather was killed, the person took his cross that he had around his neck. I knew if Charles was the killer, he would have that cross and I knew the one place he would keep it. I went to Brianna—she was the only person that knew where Charles's private safe was. I asked her, but she wouldn't tell me because she said Charles would kill her."

"I told her why I wanted to know, and she took me upstairs and in the bathroom behind the cabinet was the safe. She opened it and there in a black box was the cross. I felt empty. I held it in my hand and cried. After a while, I gave it back to her and left. I got so drunk I could hardly stand, then I called Allen and said yes."

"Chase, I want you to know if I had to do it over, I swear to you I would have never said yes, because now I know you can't fight evil with evil. I've tried to forget that night, but it's like God won't let me. Brianna was at the spa, so I knew she was going to be gone the whole day. The plan was once I was inside to go to the bathroom and go unlock the back door so Allen could sneak in. The crazy thing was it was easier than we thought it was going to be."

When I got there Charles, was in the basement putting together a go-cart for Jason. When I went in, I never locked the door behind me. What sticks out in my mind about that night was the fact that Charles was so happy. He was smiling and talking while he was working, and Charles wasn't big on talking. You know they say God always gives you a better option when you're about to do the wrong thing and he did that very thing for me that night, but I allowed hate to fill my heart. Because at that moment while I listened to him and watched him, I wanted to just run out of there, lock the door behind me and never look back."

"Instead, I stood there as I watched Allen sneak down the stairs and then put the gun to Charles head. Charles stood there not saying a word as Allen yelled and cussed. He stood there with a smile on his face. Allen asked him, "How does it feel to know you're going to die today?" I'll never forget what he said. It plays repeatedly in my head. His reply was, "Death is the only way I can be reborn." Then he looked at Allen as if to say, 'do it' and Allen shot him."

Chase sat there for a minute, taking in everything that James had said. Then he got up and he looked at James with an angry expression. "I'll get all this typed up then you'll need to sign it, but I have to say this, or it'll eat at me for the rest of my life. You sit here like a man full of regret and remorse. The sad thing is it's all fake, because regardless of what Charles did to you, it had nothing to do with Brianna and you sat back and watched her go to prison and said nothing. You allowed her to sit in prison for half her life and still you did nothing. That's not regret or remorse. If it wasn't for Jason wanting to know what really happened to his father and him ending up dead, you still would have done nothing!"

Then Chase walked out, and I thought about what he said and he was so right. He could've said something a long time ago when Jason first told him he was trying to find out about Charles's death. Then maybe Jason would still be alive today. When Chase came in and got me, I was angry, too. I wanted to talk to James, but Chase said it wasn't a good idea. I waited for Chase at his desk.

As I was standing there, Alicia and her mother were on their way to see James and as she passed, she stopped and looked at me. "I really hope you're happy, you've managed to ruin everyone's life." I looked at her for a second because I couldn't believe she really had the nerve to say that to me. I said, "Happy, no. Sickened and saddened? Your dad had a choice and he made the wrong one, and because of it four people lost their lives. For some reason, you seem to think just because he's your dad he shouldn't have to atone for what he did."

"You know, Leia, I think you live in this fantasy world like you're Miss Goody Two Shoes or some shit. Hello! Your husband was a drug dealer he sold crack! Your real mother was a whore and a drug dealer and don't get me started about Charles! Finally, Tee! I'm not even going there. My father's a good man. He doesn't deserve this and if it wasn't for Charles, he wouldn't have been in this whole mess in the first place."

She started to walk away, but I grabbed her arm and I stepped close in her face because I wanted her to know I meant every word I was about to say. "You're right, Jason was a drug dealer and Brianna was as well. She might even have been a whore, but your father is worse than them all, because he's a coward and by the way he was also a drug dealer. Oh, I forgot, it was only because he was trying to be close to Charles! Wow, that's really some stupid shit. Then instead of being a man and standing up to Charles, he did what any coward would do...he just complied. He allowed Allen to use him to help him kill Charles, but again he has excuses for that too. And let's not forget that he sat back and did nothing to help Brianna or Jason. Honey, good men don't do the things your father did, so please remember this if you don't remember anything else when you live in a glass house, don't throw stones."

I let her arm go and I walked away, this time not sad that we weren't friends anymore because she showed me who she really was and how she really felt. Nana always said you're either right or your wrong; there's no in between. When you're wrong, be woman enough to face what you've done. Alicia knows that James is wrong and instead of being real, she's choosing to blame everyone else just like James.

I turned and looked at Chase and he could tell I was ready to go. He headed toward where my mother was sitting, and she stood up and gave me a hug. On the way home as I looked out of the window, I didn't feel this sense of sadness that had surrounded me since Jason was killed. I felt whole again, like everything was going to be OK. That now Jason could rest, and I could move on.

When we got to Sandra's, I got out of the car with my mother and gave her a big hug. I know she wanted to be home, but with Lance still running around she had to stay at Sandra's. I watched her until she got inside, then I got back in the car. Chase reached over and grabbed my hand as I was still looking at Sandra's house. "Leia, she'll be all right." I squeezed his hand and turned and looked at him and smiled. "I know; I was just thinking how lucky I am to have her as a mother." He smiled back at me, "You sure are" he said.

As we drove off and made our way back to his house. As soon as we got in the door I fell on the couch and let out a loud sigh. I felt relieved that it was almost over, and once Lance was caught, it was going to be done.

"Chase, what do you usually do after you solve a case?" Before I got my sentence out good, he came in the living room holding two shot glasses and a bottle of Remy. He set up two shots, I looked at him, grabbed one of the shot glasses, and took it to the head. "Damn, girl I didn't think you had it in you!"

"Please, you know this is my drink, so you better watch out!" We had a few more shots than I sat back on the couch Chase sat back, too.

I smiled, Chase asked "What are you thinking about?"

I replied "Nothing, I am just glad this is all over."

Chase looked at me and said, "I am too, but then again I am not." He turned to look at me. I asked, "Why aren't you happy this is over?"

He sat up, poured another shot, and took it to the head, then he sat back and looked at me. "I'll miss seeing you every day."

I took my hand and brushed it across his cheek. "Who said you'll stop seeing me?" I reached over and put my lips to his and as we kissed, I felt like this was right. I wasn't confused about us anymore. I planned to take it slow, but I didn't want to lose him again. I realized that I'll always love Jason and he will be with me forever, but I also know that a part of my heart was loving Chase the whole time I was with Jason. I wanted to build on that and see where it goes. We laid on the couch and I waited until

Chase feel asleep. I slid off the couch, went and washed my face and

grabbed his keys and went to the cemetery. I needed to talk to Jason.

As I pulled up to the section where Jason was buried there was a

car parked there already. I got out and as I walked to the grave site, I could

see someone standing in front of his grave. As I got closer, I could see it

was Brianna. She turned and looked at me with tears running down her

face. I walked up to her and gave her a big hug. We hugged for a while;

then we just stood there looking at both graves. Jason was buried next to

his father; I thought that's where he'd want to be. Charles wasn't a great

person, but he was Jason's father and he loved him. We left the graveyard

and met at a diner. When I slid on the seat across from her, she was

smiling.

"You're so beautiful." She stopped and tears filled her eyes. "I

want you to know how much I wanted you I would cry myself to sleep at

night thinking about you. Like I told you before I was forced to have the

boys, but I wanted to have you not for me, but for your dad. All he talked

about was having a baby and I knew that your mother could not have any

more children. Then I had you, and the nurse put you in my arms I looked

at you and I kissed your forehead and handed you to your dad. My heart

ached because I knew that I could not give you the life that your dad and

your mother could give you. I wanted you to have a family that would love and cherish you, Leia. I gave you the one thing no one ever gave me. A chance at a wonderful life and that was the only thing that gave me any joy, knowing that you were happy and truly loved."

She was in tears, and I was glad to hear that. Since the moment I found out that Brianna was my real mother, I never hated her. I felt bad for all the things she had been through. My God, I don't think I would have been able to deal with all that. I went and sat next to her and put my arm around her and kissed her on the cheek.

"I don't hate you, Breanna. I had a life most kids could only dream of. My dad was the best and he treated me like a princess. My mom was the one who showed me that you can do and be anything you want. I have truly been blessed, so I thank you for being my mother and I thank you for giving my parents the greatest gift a person could give."

On my way back to Chase's house, for the first time in a very long time, I felt like everything was going to be all right. I turned on the radio and "Keep Ya Head up" by Tupac was playing

I turned it up and smiled and said, what don't kill you, will definitely make you Stronger!

ABOUT THE AUTHOR

Tanika Fears is the mother of four children and has 3 granddaughters. Tanika currently resides in Minnesota. Tanika has studied in the field of psychology and communications, and currently works for a local non-profit. Writing has always been a safe place for Tanika. Her goal is to use her books to entertain and inspire her readers.

Made in the USA
Columbia, SC
24 August 2022

65339916R00157